SNOW TALES AND OTHER FANCIES

Stories and Pictures for Family Sharing

by **KEENAN BROOKLAND**

SNOW TALES AND OTHER FANCIES

Stories and Pictures for Family Sharing

Compiled and edited by Keenan Brookland
Art by Slate Bender

Table of Contents

THE SNOW WORLD

By Slate Bender and Keenan Brookland

"Chester, I think there's someone behind that tree," whispered Nantucket.

Chester turned to look and saw a very thin shadow in the snow. They both watched as a thin stick figure form moved slowly from behind the tree and its face appeared.

"Greetings," Chester began. "I am Chester, and this is my wife, Nantucket." Nantucket's cheeks glowed a light pink and she smiled shyly. "What is your name?"

"When I was a person my name was Dennis. I don't know what I am now." He was going to add, "And you look like a snowman, but snowmen don't talk," when Chester interrupted with another question.

"That brings me to an urgent question," said Chester. "How did you get here? I don't remember seeing you on the Waiting List."

"Waiting List? I never heard of it. I don't know how I got here, or how I turned into...this," and the stick creature gestured to himself.

"Hmmm," mused Chester. "Very peculiar. Something seems to have gone wrong here. If you don't know how you got here, then I wonder who does?"

"I was just climbing a tree in the woods when suddenly I felt very light-headed. I decided to come down, but by the time I got down I looked like this. And then I saw you."

"I'm going to have to bring this up with the Spirit of the Snow."

Dennis knitted his very thin brows. "Would you please explain this to me from the beginning?"

Nantucket whispered something to Chester. Chester said, in warm tones, "Cheer up now, Dennis. Why don't you come with us and have a nice cup of coffee, and then we'll sort this all out."

Dennis thought of a snowman drinking coffee and suddenly burst out laughing. "How can you drink coffee? Oh, that's funny! Good joke!" He laughed and kicked his little stick feet in the snow.

When his laughter had subsided, Chester said, "What was so funny?"

"If you drank coffee you would melt!" Dennis exclaimed.

"That's an absurd idea. I don't know why I should melt. I drink coffee all the time. Come now, let's go get some." He motioned to Dennis to move towards him.

Dennis stood up, but said, "How are you going to go anywhere?"

Chester looked puzzled. "The same way anyone else does. I'll just go. What is the problem with that?"

"You don't have any feet," Dennis pointed out. "Or legs, for that matter. How will you walk?"

"Good Heavens, you don't need feet and legs to go somewhere. Watch." He took Nantucket's stick hand and they began gliding away. "Follow us!"

Dennis scrambled along behind saying, "How do you do that?"

Nantucket giggled.

Dennis looked at his form. "In fifth grade we learned about the skeleton and the muscles and all that stuff, which is what makes your body stand up and do things. Hey! How am I walking without all that stuff? I'm just a bunch of lines and I'm walking! How can that be?"

Chester said to Nantucket, "We're going to have to get to the bottom of this."
To Dennis he said, "Just don't worry about it for now. We'll answer all your questions for you once we've had a chance to talk to the Spirit of the Snow."

"I thought we were going to have coffee!" said Dennis.

"We are. There's the Coffee Stand," said Chester.

Dennis looked in the direction that Chester was pointing, and there was a coffee stand with a little man in it. It was standing alone amidst snow and trees.

"Hey, that wasn't there before. At least I didn't see it," he said.

"Coffee Stands are usually there when you want them and don't clutter up the place the rest of the time," said Chester.

"Look, there's a real man in it!" said Dennis. "Where I come from, that's what people look like!"

Nantucket and Chester turned and looked hard at him. "Oh my!" they said to each other.

"What do you mean? What's the matter?" asked Dennis, mildly frightened.

"This is becoming a serious matter. Let's remain calm, however. I'm sure there's a logical explanation for all this." Chester tossed a large money bag on the ground in front of him, which he seemed to extract out of thin air, and motioned to the man in the Coffee Stand. Nantucket went up close to him with a concerned look on her face and whispered something to him. He paused briefly and said, "Yes, I know. There's nothing we can do

COFF
HOT
$

but go to the Spirit of the Snow about this." Nantucket drew away and he continued placing his order.

"Do you like Snickerdoodle Coffee?" he asked Dennis.

"I thought Snickerdoodles were cookies, not coffee," said Dennis.

"Well, do you like it?"

"Sure. I guess so," said Dennis.

"Very good." Chester ordered three Snickerdoodle coffees and they drank together quietly. It tasted just like Snickerdoodle cookies. Dennis watched closely to see if they would melt, even a little bit, but they seemed to enjoy the coffee while remaining as snowman-like as ever.

When they had finished, Chester turned to Nantucket and said, "Do you suppose it would be best to fly or should we take the Light Rail?"

Nantucket whispered something to him and then he said, "All right, the Light Rail it is. Come along, Dennis."

The three of them glided around a clump of trees and over to a set of train tracks. "You first," said Chester to Dennis.

"What do you want me to do?"

"Step aboard," replied Chester, gesturing toward the set of train tracks.

"Wait!" cried Nantucket. "The light is yellow."

Chester and Dennis looked over at the light posted a few feet down the track and it was indeed yellow. A second later three snowmen glided by on the track, singing and making merry as they traveled. Two of them waved large mugs of coffee and the third held up a music book which he viewed through his spectacles. When they had passed, the light turned white.

Nantucket said to Dennis, "Just hop on and lean forward a little."

Dennis hopped and landed with both feet on one rail. His feet immediately started gliding down the rail and he almost fell backwards, but then caught his balance. Soon he was smoothly speeding along.

If he'd had hair, Dennis was sure it would have been flying out behind him as he raced down the Light Rail. He must have been going at least fifty miles an hour. He finally realized it was not likely that he would fall and started to have a good time. He could hear Chester and Nantucket laughing behind him and occasionally singing a short verse.

Suddenly he saw that there was an abrupt end to the land ahead on the horizon. He turned back to Nantucket in alarm and said, "What's that?"

"The End of the World," she replied.

The Light Rail did not end at that point, but continued on right into thin air. Before he had time to ask another question, they had arrived at the End of the World and went speeding along the tracks into space. Dennis screamed and grabbed Nantucket's twig arm.

"Close your eyes and we'll soon be there," said Nantucket. Dennis closed his eyes, but then he felt himself falling backwards and screamed again. The track had turned upwards straight into the air, and they were speeding straight up along with it. Nantucket held onto him with both her twig arms and said, "We're almost there now."

A few seconds later they turned upright again and came to a stop. Dennis opened his eyes and saw they had arrived in front of a huge castle. They glided over the drawbridge and into the courtyard. Snow lay in drifts all around and covered the evergreens and courtyard walls. A small pond was frozen over and looked perfect for ice skating. Dennis ran over to it and began to skate around on it.

"This way!" said Chester, and Dennis ran back over to enter the castle with them.

The inside of the castle looked very much like the outside, complete with snow and trees. By this time Dennis had stopped being surprised at the odd surroundings. He simply took it all in as he followed Chester and Nantucket.

Chester pointed to a spiraling staircase and said to Dennis, "I think it's best that you go alone."

Dennis climbed the staircase, and after counting about fifty turns he was puzzled as to how the castle could be so much taller inside than outside. He wasn't at all tired, though, so he kept climbing.

After fifty more turns he arrived at the doorway to a chamber. He entered and found a Knight in full armor sitting at a desk by candle light. The Knight rose and said, "Oh, there you are! Did you have a good trip?"

"Once I got used to it."

"Very good. But let me introduce myself. I am the Spirit of the Snow, or Sir Fife. I do apologize for the error that brought you here." Sir Fife shook his head in amazement. "You seem to have stumbled upon the exact location in your world that I am using to keep tabs on it. I have been there, you know, and have some fond memories. You must have a very similar wavelength to mine or you would not have ended up here."

"Where is here?" asked Dennis.

"This is one of many worlds. I am in charge of keeping this one in order. It's fairly small as worlds go, and beings come and go. That is a concept you are not familiar with, is it?" Sir Fife didn't wait for Dennis to answer, but continued to speak.

"Some very evil character got loose in your world and it's in quite a mess. Many of those here, such as Chester and Nantucket, have heard rumors about your world and how much Divine Intervention has been required there to save fallen beings."

"When were you in my world?" asked Dennis.

"Oh my, it's been a few of your years, I suppose. You may recognize my armor as belonging to a time and place there. I understand the Round Table became the subject of many legends. I considered Knighthood my part in trying to lend a hand there, but I wasn't really cut out for that sort of thing."

"Oh, well I don't blame you," said Dennis, "but how do I get home to my world?"

"That's easy enough," said Sir Fife. "When you're ready, just step into that location and intend to be back in your world." Sir Fife pointed to a dim corner of the chamber.

"I'd better get home," said Dennis, "before my mother worries, but can I come back again?"

"Certainly," said Sir Fife. "You are most welcome, sir."

"Can I bring my friend, Gaila? She would like this."

"I don't see why not. Mum's the word, though. This is just for the two of you, or I will have to seal the entry point. Take these passes to show when you return." Sir Fife handed him two large snowflakes. "They will turn into paper in your world. Protect them!"

"I will. Thank you Sir Fife, and I will see you again soon!" He felt Sir Fife smiling through his visor at him all the way back home.

"Ouch!" cried Gaila.

Dennis had that light-headed feeling again. His eyes focused and he saw that he was in the tree in the woods behind his own back yard. His foot was pinning Gaila's ankle against the crook of a branch.

Dennis almost fell out of the tree when Gaila's scream pierced the air. He caught himself and steadied Gaila, too, just in time to keep them from tumbling out of the tree together.

"You scared me," she scolded. "How did you sneak up on me so fast?"

"I've been in another world," he told Gaila.

"What does that have to do with anything?" she asked. "You're always daydreaming."

"Come on down and I'll tell you everything."

Dennis and Gaila clambered back down to the ground. Dennis checked in with his mother, but found that it wasn't even dinner time yet. He figured time must run differently in the Snow World. He and Gaila put a quick snack together for themselves and went back out into the yard for a long conference.

It took a while for Gaila to get the idea that he was not kidding or playing a game, but she was excited once she understood.

"The Spirit of the Snow really said I could come, too?" she asked, wide-eyed.

"Yes!" said Dennis. He pulled the snowflake passes out of his pocket. One was light blue with iridescent sparkles and the other was metallic red. "Which one do you want?" he said.

She chose the blue one. "Now what do we do?" she asked.

Dennis opened his mouth but suddenly realized he didn't know. Sir Fife had said to present the passes when he returned, but had not really explained how to return.

"Sir Fife talked about the entry point. Oh! It must be in the tree, because I was in the tree right before and right after I went to the Snow World."

They walked over to the tree, which was after all their favorite tree for climbing, and had a brief argument over who ought to go first. Then they had another argument as to whether they should approach the entry point by climbing above it from the side and slipping down into it, or by just poking their heads boldly up into it. This led to an argument about the exact location of the entry point.

"Dennis!" yelled his mother. "Dinner time!"

"Oh no," groaned Gaila. They prepared to part for the evening, knowing that they had homework after dinner and school the next day.

"Maybe we can meet in the middle of the night," suggested Dennis.

"Well," said Gaila, "we don't know for sure how to get there yet so it would be better to get a good night's sleep so we can think better. Don't you think so? Hey! You'd better not go without me! Do you promise?"

"All right, I promise," said Dennis.

Dennis tossed and turned through hundreds of dreams that night, feeling as if he did no sleeping. He didn't realize he was actually fast asleep the whole time. At one point Sir Fife appeared in his dream and gave him a friendly tip: "Position yourself at the entry point and intend to move into our world." Dennis woke up abruptly, feeling it had been very real, yet he was in bed asleep, so how could it have been real? He promised himself he would not forget the tip, just in case, and dropped off to sleep again.

After school the next day, he and Gaila went again to the tree. They climbed and positioned themselves on the limb where Dennis had been yesterday.

"Okay, Gaila....NOW. Think of the Snow World."

"Dennis, I feel so dizzy.... I think I'm falling!" wailed Gaila.

"Just keep holding my arm—" Dennis began, but before he finished the sentence they were standing in the snow and not falling at all. Gaila was holding his stick arm and laughing at his appearance, which he found a bit annoying.

"Do you have your pass?" he asked her.

"Right here," she said, waving it.

"It wouldn't hurt to show our passes right now," said Dennis. "Maybe someone will see us." He held his red snowflake above his head, waving it from side to side. Gaila did the same with her blue snowflake.

For as far as they could see there was nothing but snow in sight and they began to feel silly. Dennis turned slowly around, searching for any signs of life, and Gaila followed him. Behind them they found a small stand of very thin, leafless trees. Their hands dropped gradually to their sides and all waving of the passes subsided. They stared dumbly at the trees for a few seconds, when suddenly a snowman moved out from behind one of them.

"That's impossible," Gaila whispered. "There's no way such a fat snowman could have been hiding behind such a thin tree."

"Wave your pass," he said, prodding her with his stick elbow.

They waved their passes excitedly and the snowman tipped his hat to them.

"It's Chester!" cried Dennis. He headed toward Chester at a run and Gaila was right behind him.

"Greetings!" said Chester to both of them. He removed his top hat and had them both put their snowflakes in the hat. He handed the hat to Dennis, then turned back toward the thin trees.

"They're here!" he shouted happily. "Come out and meet Dennis and Gaila!"

Nantucket emerged next, wearing a pretty pink scarf.

They watched in amazement as snowmen emerged from behind each of the thin trees. Many of them were wearing top hats and tipped them at Dennis and Gaila. It was altogether a very dapper display.

"Snow people," Chester announced, "Dennis and Gaila have tickets to the ballet. Let there now be a performance of the Snowcracker Sweet."

The snowmen behind him murmured phrases of approval and Chester ushered them over to the theater entrance.

"I know that wasn't here before," said Gaila to Dennis as she gazed at the ornate theater door that was now before them.

"Tickets please," said the snowman at the door.

Dennis and Gaila looked at each other. "We don't have tickets to the ballet," Gaila told the snowman mournfully.

The snowman chuckled and said, "How clever of you to hide them in Chester's hat and pretend not to have a ticket! Chester told us you would be amusing!"

"Oh!" said Gaila, and quickly retrieved her snowflake to hand to the snowman at the door. They went through the doorway into a large outdoor theater, framed prettily by two rows of fir trees. The stage was very grand, but there were only two seats for the audience.

An usher appeared with a quaint lantern and said, "May I help you find your seats?"

Dennis was about to say no when Gaila said, "Why thank you, sir. But may I ask why you have only two seats? Surely this ballet must be in great demand."

"Indeed it is. Usually we have no audience at all because everyone insists on dancing in the ballet. We do, however, have two seats for just such occasions as this." Dennis and Gaila looked at each other in mutual surprise.

The usher lit their way until they were safely in their seats. "One more thing," said Gaila to the usher. "Who are the dancers?"

"I believe you met them a few moments ago, milady," he replied.

"I didn't see any ballet dancers," she said.

"Chester and Nantucket will dance the lead roles, accompanied by the Tree Troupe. Did you not see them tipping their hats to you, milady?" he asked.

"How will they ever wear toe slippers?" she wondered.

"Enjoy the show," the usher said crisply as he snuffed out his lantern and returned from wherever he had come.

The curtain began to open and tiny white sparkles illuminated the stage gradually. Chester and Nantucket glided out from opposite ends of the stage and met in the middle while Dennis and Gaila applauded loudly.

The music began, starting as a slow, lilting melody while the lights were still low and turning gradually into what seemed a rousing Russian folkdance, punctuated by sharp cracks and strokes of variously colored light each time another snowman entered the stage.

"They're flying!" exclaimed Gaila. Dennis and Gaila applauded wildly as the snowmen took to the air, circling and patterning with amazing rapidity and grace. The stage seemed to explode in a thousand bright colors and then all was black. It was so quiet that Dennis and Gaila were afraid to clap.

A sweet, harplike music began and the lights went up again. Candies and cookies fell from the sky, floating slowly as if they were feathers, then landing all about and upon Dennis and Gaila.

The snowmen were doing a three-dimensional circle dance about twenty feet above them. Dennis and Gaila leaned back to enjoy the sky dance as their seats moved into a reclining position.

One by one the snowmen danced off into the night sky, and then it was daylight again. The seats moved back into upright position and Dennis and Gaila left the theater.

Chester and Nantucket were waiting for them outside.

"What a wonderful, wonderful ballet!" exclaimed Gaila.

"It was great!" said Dennis.

"Why thank you," said Chester.

Nantucket's cheeks turned a delicate rose and she said, "It was just a little something we threw together for you. I'm glad you liked it!"

"I hope you don't mind that I gathered up some of the sweets in your hat," said Dennis to Chester.

"Not at all," said Chester. "That was the plan. You can take those back with you."

"Thank you!" replied Dennis.

"We're going to hop into the tub for a little soak," said Nantucket. "Would you like to join us?"

The four of them set off toward a field of spruce trees and soon came upon a stone patio surrounded by a low brick wall. Near one edge of the brick wall was a circular, steaming tub of water. Nantucket was about to hoist herself into it when Gaila ran up to her and embraced her, crying, "Please don't!"

"My dear, whatever is the matter?" asked Nantucket.

"Don't you see? You will melt if you go into that hot water!" Gaila cried.

"Calm yourself, little creature," said Chester. "Will you explain this idea of melting to us now so we can clear it up once and for all?"

"Melting is what happens when snow or ice gets warm and turns into a liquid," explained Dennis.

"What is a liquid?" asked Nantucket.

"It's wet, like water; like coffee!" said Dennis, knowing they would understand coffee.

"So you think that we will turn into coffee if we get into the tub?" asked Chester.

"No," said Dennis. "When snow melts—snow is what you are made of—it turns into water. Water is like coffee except it is clear and cool and has no flavor. Then when water gets really hot it turns into steam, which goes into the air and is invisible."

"What an odd idea!" said Nantucket.

Nantucket and Chester sailed into the tub and were soon enjoying a soak, a Snickerdoodle coffee and each other's company. Dennis and Gaila joined them for a short time, then jumped out and took a walk around the patio.

When they returned to the tub, Chester said, "Look at what I've made! Is that melting?"

Dennis and Gaila looked where he was pointing, just outside the tub, and saw three large blocks of ice, which were indeed melting and forming a puddle of water on the patio.

"That looks like my cat," said Gaila, startled. There was a cat hopping from one of the ice blocks to another. "That's funny... I was just thinking about him when we came to the patio."

"That explains it," said Chester. "Dennis, why don't you and Gaila visit Sir Fife and ask him all your questions?"

"Is he the one in the Castle?" asked Gaila.

"That's him," said Dennis.

"How do we get to the Light Rail from here, Chester?" asked Dennis.

"Actually, I thought you'd prefer to fly today. Am I right?" answered Chester.

Dennis and Gaila's eyes widened. "Do you have an airport here, too?" Dennis asked.

"Heavens, no! Here, I'll show you how it's done." He leapt out of the tub and guided them

to an open spot away from the patio. "You'll need a stick for maneuvering, of course," he continued, and handed them each a candy cane. Hold it out in front of you, nice and steady. That's right! When you're ready to take off, just pull back on the stick! Always face the direction you want to go. Have a pleasant journey!"

Chester glided back over to Nantucket. Dennis and Gaila braced themselves and took off. They rose so quickly into the sky that it was quite dizzying. Soon they were high enough for Dennis to spot the End of the World.

"Turn this way, Gaila!" he yelled. They sailed off in that direction, speeding much faster than Dennis had gone on the Light Rail. Dennis was momentarily confused because he couldn't see the Light Rail tracks, but he remembered that Sir Fife's castle was up, so they flew straight up and arrived at the castle in no time.

"Push forward on the stick, Gaila!" yelled Dennis. They landed gracefully on the castle grounds.

Together they wound up the long stairway, all one hundred turns, and arrived in the candle lit chamber.

"How nice to see you again!" said Sir Fife.

"Hello, Sir Fife," said Dennis. "This is Gaila."

Gaila said, "Thank you for giving me a pass to the Snow World."

"You are very welcome," he said. "And now let's clear up a few things. You realize, don't you, that things are a bit different here?"

Dennis and Gaila laughed. "More than a bit," said Gaila.

"Well, yes and no. Living here is like playing a game of make-believe, except that whatever you make up becomes real for you and everyone else here."

"Oh," said Dennis. "I wish I could live in a world like this."

"Me, too," echoed Gaila.

"And that probably has a great deal to do with why you're here. Not everyone in your world would feel safe in a place where their thoughts could be seen by others. But enough of that. I've got quite a bit to do today, so why don't you two run along and see the sights?"

"Sir Fife, can we please be snow people like everyone else?" asked Gaila.

Sir Fife tilted his head to one side and then to the other. "I don't see why not," he replied. "Actually, that's a splendid idea! I'll let Chester and Nantucket know right away. They'll be ready when you get there. Off you go, now.

"Did I tell you there's a shortcut back to the Snow World through that window?" said Sir Fife.

A very tall tree with an extremely spindly top was within reach of the window ledge. Dennis jumped onto it and Gaila followed him. They climbed down the tree carefully at first.

"Did you look down, Gaila?" said Dennis after a few moments. "This is a very strange tree."

Gaila looked and saw that the tree got wider and wider until it was so wide that she couldn't see the edges. "Let's slide!" she said.

They let go and slid down, down and further down for at least thirty seconds. Finally the edge of the tree appeared far below them and Gaila screamed. They were rapidly gaining speed and it looked as if they would be propelled out into empty space with no sign of any ground below the tree.

They both began yelling at the top of their lungs and holding their stick arms up in the air, much as children do in this world when they are on the roller-coaster and know they are having a safe ride.

At last they were going at least a hundred times faster than anything on earth, they were sure, but it wasn't uncomfortable at all because they were stick people. They whooshed off the end of the tree and went sailing into the air. Within seconds they saw trees and snow beneath them, but instead of falling down, they began going slower and slower until they were floating gently toward the ground and lighted on their feet with no more impact than if they had walked down a stair.

"I see you took the shortcut," said Chester from behind them. They turned and saw that Chester and Nantucket were standing together at a basin that looked very much like a birdbath. In it, however, was a small snowman-like form, complete except for carrot nose, scarf and cap. Chester was just getting ready to place the cap on its head.

"This is yours, Gaila. It's almost done," said Chester. He slid the red and white stocking cap onto the little snowgirl's head and put in her carrot nose. Nantucket wrapped a green scarf around the snowgirl's neck.

"Go ahead. Try it on!" urged Nantucket.

"It's not like it's clothes," said Gaila.

Chester said, "Pretend you're that snowgirl."

Gaila pretended, as best she could, and instantly she had the strange sensation of being big and round. Dennis watched in awe as the little snowgirl expanded and came to life.

"I did it!" said Gaila, as the snowgirl.

Chester and Nantucket made a snowman form for Dennis, too, except that his wore a top hat instead of a stocking cap. Once he had put on his form, Chester and Nantucket suggested they go on the Scenic Route.

"What's that?" asked Dennis.

"A Light Rail journey around our world. It starts over there. Have fun!" Chester was pointing to the Light Rail tracks which had conveniently appeared again.

Dennis and Gaila glided over to the tracks. "It's kind of tricky keeping your balance at first," said Dennis, "but you'll get the hang of it in a few seconds."

"Let's go together, side by side," suggested Gaila. "You can hold my hand in case I start to fall."

"Okay," said Dennis, and they hopped onto the track, one on each rail, and held hands. Nothing happened.

"Suddenly they were jolted forward as they started to move. They nearly lost their hats as they continued down the rail in fits and starts.

"It's much smoother in single file," said Chester to them, so Dennis hopped over to Gaila's rail and soon they were speeding gracefully along.

THE SCENIC ROUTE

By Slate Bender and Keenan Brookland

"I don't know why they call this the Scenic Route," said Gaila to Dennis, who was flying along the Light Rail in front of her. "There's no scenery. And if there was, you'd be going too fast to see it."

"What do you mean, no scenery?" yelled Dennis, turning back to look at her. "Look at all this snow!"

"That doesn't count," she said. "There's snow everywhere. This is a whole world of snow. I'm getting tired of it!"

"If you look far away," said Dennis, "you can see some colors on the horizon. Have you ever seen purple snow? Or reddish-gold snow? Look over there!"

Gaila turned her head to the left, where Dennis was pointing. Splashes of colored light streamed over the snow in the distance, almost too far away to see.

"I wonder what's happening over there?" said Gaila.

In the next moment the two of them were standing among gently rolling mounds of snow. The Light Rail was nowhere in sight. Colored light swirled close to the ground like eddies of dust in a wind storm. A snow couple stood not far from them. The snowman was wearing a black top hat and the snowlady wore a red cap with white trim and a white puff on the long and pointed end of her cap. They wore bright red woolen scarves that matched.

Dennis and Gaila watched as the snowman guided the snowlady over to a very particular spot, his arm around her shoulder, while with the other arm he gestured skyward. The swirling colors bolted up from the ground and arced over the sky, followed by a rush of sparkles that glimmered in the light of the rainbow.

"Oh, Meriwether! It's beautiful!" said the snowlady.

"Why thank you, Lucille," he answered.

Meriwether and Lucille looked over at Dennis and Gaila and greeted them cordially by name. "How nice of you to visit us," said Lucille.

"Can I try it?" asked Gaila.

"Certainly," said Meriwether.

Gaila glided over to one of the pools of swirling colors and swept her arm upward toward the sky. A stream of colors started up and then fluttered out crookedly in every direction, like ribbons curling and flying wildly.

"Try it again," said Lucille, "but don't let go this time."

Gaila fared better the second time, making an arc of about 100 yards with all the colors perfectly parallel.

"Very nice!" said Lucille. "Just needs some more ooomph."

Dennis tried his hand at it also, but they both realized they'd need more practice before they could make all-the-way-across-the-sky rainbows like the one Meriwether had made. Dennis turned around and there was the Light Rail, even though it hadn't been there last time he looked. He showed Gaila and they hopped on, waving good-bye to Meriwether and Lucille.

"I wonder if there are any castles here," said Dennis, "or if Sir Fife's castle beyond the End of the World is the only one."

In the twinkling of a snowflake they were standing before a great castle. Gaila ran inside while Dennis ran around the perimeter, exploring.

Inside the castle Gaila found a wooden table with a small bouquet of dried flowers on it. She sat down and wondered what it would be like to be a medieval princess. Five ladies-in-waiting walked in from an inner room and groomed her snow hair, then placed a beautiful pink medieval headdress upon her head, cone-shaped with a satiny trail of cloth flowing from the point. The ladies bowed courteously as they departed. Trumpets sounded outside the castle and a steady stream of knights began coming through the doorway, one at a time, bowing very low and paying homage to Lady Gaila, then stepping back outside.

It was amusing at first, and very flattering, but Gaila grew curious as to what had become of Dennis when the sky darkened and stars came out. She noticed that a torch now burned above the doorway where the last of the knights had just departed. Dennis bounded through the door, brandishing a very large candy cane.

"Look what I've found!" he said. "There's a whole garden of these outside. Would you like to go flying with me?"

"Oh yes!" cried Gaila. "I've had enough of knights in creaking armor. Let's have some fun."

They tried all manner of aerobatics and did spirals downward at impossible speeds without ever crashing, following the instructions Chester had given them for their trip to Sir Fife's castle. Flying in an airplane is one thing, but you really can't imagine the pure excitement of flying with nothing but a candy cane stick until you've done it yourself.

At last Dennis and Gaila floated down for a landing, having had enough flying for the moment. They saw the Light Rail, and hastened over to it as soon as they had stowed their candy cane sticks neatly in the garden where they had found them.

"Wait!" said Dennis, and he held out his arm in front of Gaila. "The light's yellow and we'll have to wait, because that means someone is coming."

Gaila looked down the track a few feet and sure enough, a light post had appeared next to the Light Rail while they were putting away their candy canes. The light was yellow. A few seconds later a wonderful old-fashioned sleigh came coasting down the tracks at the slowest speed they had yet seen in the Snow World. Chester and Nantucket were seated in the sleigh, enjoying a game of chess. Their chess board was red and green instead of red and black, and each piece was a snowman (or snow castle or snow horse, as the case may be). Chester and Nantucket were quite caught up in their game, but they did look up and wave at Dennis and Gaila as they passed.

As soon as the light turned white, Dennis and Gaila boarded the Light Rail and continued on the Scenic Route.

"I've seen trees here," said Gaila, "but I haven't seen any flowers growing. For the Snow World to be perfect it just has to have flowers."

No sooner had she finished the sentence when they noticed huge fields of flowers on either side of the Light Rail tracks. These were not ordinary flowers, however.

"I can't believe it!" said Dennis. "Snow Flowers!"

Instead of green, the stems and leaves were translucent, shimmering with reflected pastel colors and veined with gold and silver. The blooms were miniature snowmen, smiling and curious. Each had a stocking cap of a distinctive color, and arranged in groups of colors they were quite striking.

"How do you do?" a group of them said to Dennis and Gaila as they sped through the field. Another group was singing something that sounded vaguely like "For He's a Jolly Good Fellow," while yet another group was waving, bending, diving and spinning as if in a wind storm.

"You wouldn't think it would be so fun to be a flower," said Dennis. To his amazement, the snow flowers laughed merrily as soon as he had spoken. In one fell swoop they all jumped out of the ground—all that he could see, at any rate—soared into the sky and turned into snow planes with carrot nose propellers.

"Why don't we watch a movie?" suggested Dennis.

They found themselves standing in front of a theater. They looked at the marquis and saw that "Gone With the Spring" was showing, starring Chester as "Snow Butler" and Nantucket as "Starlet Snowhara." They were soon weeping as the snow soldiers were losing the war and facing a world without snow.

Chester uttered the final line, "Frankly my dear, I don't believe in melting," and Dennis and Gaila gave them a standing ovation.

Back on the Light Rail, Dennis had a thought. "I wonder if they have Christmas here? What a perfect place to have Christmas!"

They found themselves off the Light Rail once again and approaching a settlement of igloos. A very nice snowman standing by a light post tipped his hat to them.

"Santa's in town, you know. Right that way," he said. He gestured down the snow boulevard.

Dennis and Gaila glided onward. Along the way they noticed that one of the igloos was decorated with beautiful pastel lights. A snow child peeked out of the igloo next door to it and smiled at them. Occasionally they passed another snow person or two who were out for a stroll.

At the end of the boulevard was a forest cottage, and seated outside, enjoying the fresh air, was that dear old man himself; the very same one who frequents the malls and storybooks of Earth.

"Ho, ho ho!" exclaimed Santa. "I've been waiting all year for a letter from you, and you came in person instead! Welcome to my little cottage. This is where I vacation. Would you like some Snickerdoodle coffee? We also have sparkling cider and snow-fizz, but I often forget that. Snickerdoodle coffee is so much the custom lately. I think I'll have a snow-fizz, myself, just for the fun of it. That was quite a popular drink back when Birth of a CarboNation was playing in the theater."

"I'll have one of those, too," said Gaila.

"Me, too,"' said Dennis.

Sipping the fizzy drinks near Santa's vacation cottage was very pleasant. He reminded them, however, that as much as he liked seeing snow children in person, he needed them to put their requests in writing. "Letters are such wonderful things," he told them. "I especially like very, very long ones that are so long you have to roll them up and tie them with a ribbon just to keep them from running all across the floor. Would you write me one like that?"

Dennis and Gaila's eyes went wide with wonder. They had always been told to keep their letters to Santa short because only greedy little children asked for a lot of toys for Christmas.

As if he had read their thoughts, which of course he had, Santa added, "You could tell me a bit of news, you know. Make it interesting for me. Spice it up. How about it?"

"We'll get right on it, Santa," said Gaila. They went over to a little desk not far away and began writing. It was hard at first, but Dennis and Gaila solved that right away. Most children, even on Earth, are quite good at inventing "news" when life is too boring. The funny thing is that children's tales are sometimes much closer to the truth than whatever in the world adults are thinking and saying. If you're not sure how that can be, then your only hope is to read the very long letter that Dennis and Gaila wrote to Santa about the Fleet Cats.

THE FLEET CATS LETTER

By Slate Bender and Keenan Brookland

While they were on the Scenic Route in the Snow World, Dennis and Gaila decided they would compose the longest and most interesting letter Santa had ever received. After all, he had been delivering toys to boys and girls every Christmas for years, giving them exactly what they wanted without ever requiring anything in return. Perhaps he had received a lot of milk and cookies, but who was to know if that's what he really wanted? Dennis and Gaila had heard from his own mouth that he wanted a long letter, so they set out to give him just that.

They started writing in the afternoon and didn't know exactly how much time was passing, but they each had many empty snow-fizz glasses on the table by the time the letter was done. Here is what they wrote:

Dear Santa,

We were going to write you a letter to thank you for all the bicycles and toys and candy that you've brought us over the years, but then an amazing thing happened. We heard a whizzing sound in the sky and a flying saucer came down and landed. You always hear about Martians and flying saucers, but there were only four cats in this one.

They were not regular cats. They walked up on two feet instead of all four, they were shaped almost like humans and they talked. They wore helmets but no space suits; we don't know exactly why.

"What are you doing here?" we said in amazement to the cats.

"We were just out for a Sunday drive and must have made a wrong turn," said the tall one.

"Well if that isn't the biggest dish of gizzards I've ever heard!" said the short, fat one.

"We have an image to maintain," whispered the nervous-looking one.

"I think it's too late now," said the girl cat.

"Very well," said the first one. "We made a slight miscalculation and landed when we were supposed to orbit, and now we've blown our cover. But if you have a heart, perhaps you'd keep our visit a secret for the time being. We're from the Fleet."

"Sure," we said. "But why are you here, anyway?"

"Don't tell!" said the short, fat one.

"All right, don't tell," said Gaila. "But at least tell us your names. I'm Gaila and this is Dennis."

"I'm K'Nuber," said the tall one. "I'm in charge. And these are my ship-mates Trebble (the short, fat one), Bagatail (the nervous one), and Rondui (the girl cat). We salute you."

The four cats all began to purr at the same time, which made quite a racket.

"We're having snow-fizz," said Dennis. "Would you like some?"

"Oh no thank you," said K'Nuber. "We've got to stick with rations. Native food is not approved for us. Except Captain Crunch. Have you got any?"

We found some for them and they crunched on it very loudly, without any milk. When they finished eating we had to figure out where they would stay. Not to mention hiding the flying saucer. We'd seen the movie ET and we knew we had to hide these aliens before the scientific investigators got hold of them.

We started to get better acquainted with them after that.

"What's it like where you come from?" was our first question. K'Nuber answered first, but then each of the others spoke up, one after the other. In fact, we found they always spoke in the same order: K'Nuber, Trebble, Bagatail and Rondui.

K'Nuber said, "It's a nice place. Lots of peace and quiet. I like nothing more than walking through the door of my stylish bungalow, saying, 'Hi Kitten! I'm home' and having my wife trot over to greet me. I live a very domestic sort of life when I'm not on business or on mission."

"I admire my fellow cat citizens because they have a fine sense of duty," said Trebble. "Cats are very hygienic and orderly. We all live in very nice houses. In fact, I've heard so much about the way you people-creatures live in all kinds of houses that I'd be curious to see them. I've heard that some of you don't even have houses and live on the street but others have more than one house. I can't figure out why you would have such a silly system."

"Haven't you ever played Monopoly?" said Dennis.

"Apparently not," said Bagatail.

"We'll tell you about it later," said Gaila. "Go on."

"My favorite thing about home is lying down at night in the hills and watching the shooting mice," said Bagatail. "I won an award for spotting more than any other Fleet Cat."

"I agree that's a nice pastime," said Rondui, "but I prefer parachuting in on mice picnics. It's quite fun when they've had too much wine."

"You're not going to invade Earth are you?" asked Dennis after they had finished talking about their homeland.

"Oh no!" said K'Nuber. He looked a little hurt that we brought up the possibility. "We're just here visiting. Simple as that."

"Did you know we have cats here?" said Gaila.

"We're quite aware of that," said Trebble. "Quite aware. But you may not know that they emigrated here from our planet thousands of years ago. We are disappointed that they've taken such a passive role in your society. They seem to have devolved to some kind of pet-like creature."

"Perhaps they can be re-educated," said Bagatail, "though that would be a very risky undertaking."

"We're just here to learn. We've heard that you people-creatures like to have wars and other unpleasant mechanisms for obtaining more possessions and power. This is not what motivates cats."

"I'll say," said Dennis. "My cat sleeps most of the time."

"No doubt an escape mechanism," said K'Nuber. "It must be hard living here, being a peace-loving cat."

"The cats fight, too," said Gaila. "I heard a cat fight just last night. And once my cat came home with a scratched ear."

"Oh dear," said Trebble. "How uncat-like."

"I told you we would run into problems here," said Bagatail to K'Nuber. "I think we had better shorten our stay."

"It's not as bad as it sounds," said Dennis. "You have to look at the good side, too."

"We fully intend to do that," said Rondui in her cute girl cat voice. We were beginning to like her the best because she was the smartest, but K'Nuber was pretty nice, too.

The next thing the Fleet Cats did was to sit down for their study period. We found out that they don't go to school like humans. They have a study period every day for two hours, no matter what. It's not just when they're kittens, but every day of their whole life! At first we thought that sounded awful, but when we saw what a good time they were having, we changed our minds.

We brought them books from our own bookshelves but we had no idea what they would like to study. We brought them *The Cat in the Hat*, though we were a little afraid they might be offended. They weren't. They thought it was very funny.

We brought them some encyclopedias, thinking that would be handy. We were very surprised when they said they'd read it last year.

"How could you?" asked Gaila.

 K'Nuber said nothing and smiled.

We decided we had a lot to learn about the Fleet Cats, but we'll write you another letter when we've learned more.

Yours Forevermore,

Gaila and Dennis

"I hope Santa likes his letter," said Gaila as she signed her name with an extra squiggle for decoration. She handed the letter to Dennis, who was just finishing his fifteenth snow-fizz.

"Careful!" said Dennis sharply. "You're going to tear it." The letter was all on one very, very long piece of paper, which went down to the floor and settled into a little roll near the feet of Gaila's chair. She gently picked up the pile of paper and put it over on Dennis' side of the table.

"I'm glad we had me do the writing," said Gaila, "because you have very sloppy writing."

"But I have a better imagination," said Dennis.

"Maybe," said Gaila, doubtfully. "It doesn't matter. It's from both of us, so just sign it and then we'll look for a ribbon. Do you think Santa will feel like we spiced it up enough?"

"Are you kidding?" said Dennis. "This is a GREAT letter!"

"Why don't you put some nutmeg on it, just to be sure?" said a voice from behind them. They turned to see a lady who looked very much like Mrs. Santa Claus. She was holding a tray of spices. "He likes cinnamon and cardamom, too, but not as much."

"Oh! Is that what he meant when he said to spice it up?" said Gaila.

"Perhaps, dear," said Mrs. Claus. "But you never know."

"Why would you put spice on a letter?" said Dennis.

"Have you ever eaten an unspiced letter, my dear?" asked Mrs. Claus. "It's better than nothing at all, but why not be generous?"

Dennis and Gaila looked at each other and smiled at the thought of eating letters, but they were too well acquainted with the peculiarities of the Snow World to be very surprised.

"Where we come from," said Dennis, "no one eats letters at all. They're not edible."

Mrs. Claus considered that. "It's a matter of politeness here, I suppose. If no one can swallow what you write, what's the use of writing? We always make our letters very palatable."

"That's ingenious!" said Gaila. "What flavor is this paper?"

"Pistachio raisin," said Mrs. Claus. "That's his favorite, so we seldom have any other kind of paper here. Except when he changes his favorite, which could happen any time."

"Do you know where we can find a ribbon to tie up this letter?" asked Dennis.

"Right over there, dear, in the ribbon patch." Mrs. Claus pointed to their left. "You'd better hurry, though. Christmas is in five minutes."

"How is Santa going to get our letter and deliver everyone's presents in just five minutes?" said Dennis.

"Don't you worry about that," said Mrs. Claus. "But do be sure you remember to tell Santa what you want in your letter."

Dennis and Gaila both turned back to the table. They'd spent a great deal of time making up a Fleet Cat story for Santa, but they hadn't mentioned a single thing they wanted for Christmas.

"What should we say?" said Gaila. "I mean, Christmas is in five minutes so we don't have much time to consider this."

"I have a request," said Mrs. Claus, "if you need an idea."

"I guess we do," sighed Dennis. "What is it?"

"I think it would be delightful to get an Easter for Christmas," she said. "I've never had one. It looks nice, though, from everything I've seen."

"Oh, won't that be a sight!" said Gaila. She grabbed the pen and added to the letter:

> *P.S. Santa, may we please have an Easter for Christmas?*

Gaila grabbed Dennis by the hand and took him quickly to the Ribbon Patch, where they found a bright red ribbon. Gaila sprinkled nutmeg all over the letter, Dennis added a touch of cinnamon, and then they tied the letter up in scroll fashion with the red ribbon.

Mrs. Claus pointed at a mailbox nearby that said Santa Claus, North Pole and said, "Only 30 seconds until Christmas! Here are your stockings." She tossed them each a long sock with sparkly fur on the top. Dennis' stocking was green and Gaila's was red.

Gaila handed her stocking to Dennis and said, "Hurry and hang these up on the mantle while I mail this letter!" Dennis turned around to find a mantle right behind him, and by the time Gaila had glided to the mailbox and back there were two little beds waiting for them. They each snuggled into a bed, which was rather difficult with their snow person forms, but they managed to get under the covers with their eyes closed just before the clock struck.

THE FLEET CATS VISIT

By Slate Bender and Keenan Brookland

"Christ–mas, Christ–mas," said the snowman in the clock, instead of "cuckoo." Then he blew a few notes on a very small horn.

Dennis and Gaila were tempted to peek when they heard Santa come down the chimney, especially when they heard him exclaim, "Ho, ho, ho! What a lovely, spicy letter these two snow children sent me. The best letter I've ever received! I'm going to give them exactly what they wanted." Dennis listened closely to see if Gaila was rustling her head out from beneath the covers, because he had decided that if she looked then he would, too. Gaila, however, was listening to see if Dennis rustled his head out from beneath the covers, for the very same reason. So it turned out that neither of them peeked.

Once they'd heard Santa calling to his reindeer and wishing all a Good Night, they leapt out of their beds and grabbed their stockings from the mantle. Dennis managed to get his emptied first.

"It's an egg!" he said.

Gaila found an egg in stocking too and was looking it over very carefully. "If you look all around the egg, you might find some small writing," she said to Dennis. "Mine says something." She held it very close to her eyes and read aloud, "Open this egg carefully and sprinkle the contents lightly over the ground."

"Hey, mine says something too," said Dennis. "Throw this egg up into the air as hard as you can."

"Should we start now?" asked Gaila.

"Sure," said Dennis. He wound up for a good throw as best he could, considering that he was a snowperson with stick arms, and up went the egg. It was very pretty to watch. It drifted slowly upward, turning round and round in a way that was almost mesmerizing. The colors sparkled and shone. After a couple seconds, when they expected it to start coming back down, they were surprised to see it start speeding up, continuing up into the sky. In another couple of seconds it was gone.

"Nothing happened," said Dennis, disappointed.

"I don't call that nothing," said Gaila. "Besides, it hasn't come back down yet. Just wait." She opened her egg very carefully, cupping it in her hands and pulling on both ends until it came apart slightly. She held it out over the ground and made a sprinkling motion.

"Nothing's coming out," said Dennis.

"Maybe we just can't see it," said Gaila. "Yet." She continued to sprinkle, gliding across the snow. Dennis followed her for lack of anything better to do.

"Hey!" he shouted when he happened to glance back. "The snow is turning green behind us!"

Just then Dennis' egg came floating down from the sky. It grew larger and larger until it was very near the ground, at which point it exploded. There was no sound with the explosion, which was very odd, but pieces of the giant egg blew apart in every direction.

When all the debris had cleared, Dennis and Gaila found themselves in a totally different landscape. There was no snow at all, except for themselves, as they were still snow people. They were in a huge tulip field that stretched as far as the eye could see.

"What beautiful red tulips!" exclaimed Gaila. She began gliding through the tulips, but stopped suddenly when a saucer-shaped craft appeared in the sky. It seemed to be heading for a relatively open space near them. They ran to the edge of the clearing and watched.

The craft made a very pert landing, and five Fleet Cats leapt out in short order. Dennis and Gaila were astounded.

"Good landing, Primrose," said Spiritus. "You fly better than Growler."

"Yes, but I always take the Scenic Route," said Growler. He looked very pleased with himself.

"We had to get here in time for Easter," said Whiskers. "You always get us everywhere fifteen centuries late."

"Now, now," said Primrose. "He actually gets us places pretty well on time because he starts fifteen centuries early. Think of the experiences we've had! Especially when he went the wrong way in a one-way galaxy. He does much better than I do in asteroid belts, too."

"Hello!" shouted Whiskers to Dennis and Gaila. Whiskers had a tendency to pay attention to anything except whatever Primrose was telling him, so he was the first to notice the snow persons. "Fleet Cats at your service," he said, bowing.

"Hello!" called Dennis and Gaila back to him. They walked over to introduce themselves to the Fleet Cats.

"Is there an Easter here anywhere?" said Growler.

"Not yet," said Dennis. "But I wouldn't be surprised if it started any minute. It's looking awfully like it might."

Dennis and Gaila introduced themselves and found out the names of the Fleet Cats:

Growler, Primrose, Spiritus, Whiskers and DaphneKat. The last one was the littlest one, and very cute, too.

"How do you know an Easter when you see one?" asked Spiritus, ever practical and to-the-point.

"There would have to be Easter Baskets," said Gaila, "and maybe an Easter Egg Hunt."

"I'd like one Easter Basket, please," said DaphneKat. "The largest size."

Gaila smiled, and went running back into the thick of the tulips to see if she could find a basket. There were exactly seven beautiful baskets, just waiting. She gave DaphneKat the slightly larger one, and passed out the rest of them until everyone had a basket.

"Now we are going to have an Easter Egg Hunt," said Gaila to the assembly. "Look around everywhere and see if you can find Easter Eggs. When you find one, put it in your basket. When all the eggs are found, whoever has the most eggs is the winner!"

"I think that whoever gets the fewest eggs should be the winner," said Whiskers, "because everyone else will have more eggs already. Don't you think that would be fair?"

"Wow," said Dennis. "You don't even know what the word *winner* means."

"Sure I do," said Whiskers. "The winner is the one who gets the prize."

"Is there a prize?" said DaphneKat, perking up. "Is it KatNip by any chance?"

"I don't know if there is a prize or not," said Dennis, "but the winner is not only the one who gets the prize, but the one who deserves it because he found the most eggs. In other words, he did the best job at the Easter Egg hunt."

"I think the winner should be the one who finds the most interesting egg," said Growler. "Anybody can find an egg, but it takes talent to find an especially interesting egg."

"I think the winner should be the one who fills his basket first," said Spiritus.

"No, no," said DaphneKat. "The winner should be the one who can get the egg that gives the best chase."

"This is ridiculous!" said Dennis. "Easter Eggs don't give chase."

"That one does," said DaphneKat. Sure enough, they looked where DaphneKat was pointing and a pink Easter Egg with purple polka dots was rolling through the tulips. DaphneKat crouched low to observe it.

"Frankly," said Primrose, "I don't see why we can't have everyone win the Easter Egg Hunt. Dennis wins as soon as he has more eggs than anyone else. Spiritus wins as soon as he fills his basket. DaphneKat wins when she has caught the egg giving the most excellent chase, Growler wins when he finds the most interesting egg, and Whiskers wins when everybody else has more eggs than he has."

"What about you and Gaila?" asked Spiritus of Primrose.

"Simple," replied Primrose. "I win when the eggs start singing in my basket. What about you, Gaila?"

"I win when the eggs start dancing in my basket," said Gaila.

"It's all decided then," said Primrose. "Start!"

Every Fleet Cat and snow person got busy immediately with the Easter Egg Hunt. It was more challenging than you might have guessed.

Growler found the most boring eggs imaginable everywhere he looked. They were practically all khaki or typewriter gray. The best one he found in the first hour was white with the incomplete formula "E = ..." written on it. This got him a little bit excited.

Meanwhile DaphneKat was having trouble as well. Each time she found a frisky egg to chase, it either stopped rolling altogether and acted stone dead when she batted it, or it rolled off so rapidly that she couldn't find it again.

Whiskers was finding so many eggs so fast that he never could manage to keep his basket emptier than anybody else's. Even if he put all his eggs back and started over, he always found someone else who had fewer eggs than he did when he ran around to check.

That is probably because Gaila and Primrose kept emptying their baskets. They would fill their baskets, ask the eggs to sing and dance, and then they would have no choice but to start over again. One time Primrose's basket of eggs all said in unison, "I can't carry a tune in a bucket!" One of Gaila's baskets of eggs sprouted left feet and proceeded to step on each other's toes. Several times they got whole baskets of eggs that did absolutely nothing. Once Primrose's basket of eggs broke out into a rap song, but she didn't consider that it was singing. She promptly put them all back and started over.

Spiritus and Dennis were quite puzzled about their baskets. No matter how many eggs they found, their baskets never seemed to be as full as the others. Spiritus was distracted for a moment once, enjoying the sight of DaphneKat poised to chase a pink and yellow Easter Egg, when he happened to notice something out of the corner of his eye. He turned to look at the tulips in front of him just as they were slipping an egg out of his basket.

"Hey!" said Spiritus. "These tulips are stealing my eggs! I demand to the speak to the Gardener!"

"What's the trouble here?" said the Gardener, an old man in blue jeans who carried a hoe as if it were a scepter.

"I'm losing this Easter Egg Hunt because your flowers are taking my eggs out of the baskets as fast as I can put them in!" cried Spiritus. "That's not fair! You need to teach some manners to these blooms."

"Pardon my bloomers, sir," said the Gardener very humbly. "This is their first Easter, and they're perhaps a bit more aggressive than one might like—"

"Just tell them to give my eggs back!" said Spiritus angrily.

"I don't know if that is such a good idea, sir," said the Gardener. "They do have a temper, and it's really very uncomfortable when you've got agitated bloomers about—"

"I want my eggs back!" said Spiritus loudly.

"Me too!" said Dennis, chiming in from three rows over.

The Gardener's face tightened with distress. Spiritus noticed that the tulips not only refused to give his eggs back but began growing rapidly. In no time at all the tulips were nearly as tall as Spiritus and emitting an ominous rumble, so he conceded that the gardener had been right and said, "Never mind!" as he walked quickly in the other direction.

Each of the Easter Egg Hunt game players was just about to the point of considering that the hunt was a little too hard when the tide began gradually to turn. Growler started finding eggs with sine waves and trigonometry formulas on them, DaphneKat found eggs that would give chase for three yards before they were caught, and Gaila got one egg to tap dance to the tune of "Way Down Upon the Swanee River," as sung by an egg in Primrose's basket. The Hunt proceeded quickly from there.

It happened all in one final, grand wave: Primrose and Gaila came to the clearing with their singing and dancing eggs, Growler brought his prize egg that hovered as it defied gravity, Whiskers came with a single egg in his basket (it was a Nike), DaphneKat brought three writhing eggs captive in her basket, and Dennis and Spiritus came with baskets full to the brim. When a final count was done, Dennis had more eggs than anyone, even though Spiritus also had a completely full basket. Everybody won!

The Gardener rang the dinner bell and everyone went to sit at the table for dinner. Growler ate three helpings of everything. That's why the Fleet Cats had to wait an extra two hours before take-off. Growler had eaten so much that they were over their weight limit. Whiskers and Spiritus complained for half an hour about that, but Primrose made them play Scrabble until they forgot about it.

Primrose sat and looked at the tulips until it was time to take off. We can only guess what she was thinking. She navigated while Growler flew, so they had a very interesting lift-off. In fact, the whole tulip field lifted off with them. Dennis and Gaila waved as the Fleet Cats flew out of sight. They were surrounded again with unending vistas of snow.

"What do we do now?" asked Gaila.

"Let's catch the Light Rail!" said Dennis. Just then they heard some caroling snowmen passing by on the Light Rail, so they hopped aboard behind them, single file, and wondered where they might end up next. Gaila began thinking of the tropics, so what do you suppose happened?

FLOATING FOLKLORE

By Colette Bree

"That's a good boy," said Grandpa. Five-year-old Grant was bending over to pick up the popsicle wrapper he had dropped. He gave it to Grandpa for safekeeping.

Grant took Grandpa by the hand and tried to hurry him up a little bit. He was anxious to get out to the sand. He'd never been to the beach before.

"Will I drown, Grandpa?" said Grant, without the slightest bit of alarm.

"No, no," Grandpa said with similar objectivity. "You only drown if you go too far out in the water without knowing how to swim, or if the currents are dangerous. You and I are just going to get our toes wet for right now."

Grant followed Grandpa's lead in sitting down at the edge of the walk to take off his shoes and socks. Grandpa was slow because he was old and Grant was slow because he was young. It worked out just about right, and they set off together onto the warm sand, leaving their shoes on the edge of the walk with the socks hanging out sloppily.

"Grandpa, it's hard to walk on this sand!" complained Grant, but he was doing quite a bit better than Grandpa at making headway toward the water.

"I know," said Grandpa. "Take your time. Old Woman Sea likes it better when she gets to know you slowly. Come on back here and hold Grandpa's hand, now."

Grant reluctantly did as he was told. "Who is Old Woman Sea?" asked Grant.

"Well, now that's a difficult question, my boy," said Grandpa. "Some say she is a goddess in the deep, overseeing all the ships that sail and creatures that live in the sea. Some say she is just a figment of the imagination. *Science* doesn't like us to believe in our cherished ideas. Let's just say that she's the one who is making these waves roll on the beach, over and over and over, and she is the one who makes us feel that the sea is so beautiful we must dance through the water like this ... " and he did the tiniest little snippet of a jig in the water as it just lapped over his feet.

Grant had to imitate it right away. "Is she making me do this, Grandpa?"

"That's right, my boy. But it could have been you doing it."

"Yeah, I think it was me, Grandpa."

They walked along the wet sand and danced every time the waves hit their feet, until Grandpa was so exhausted he had to head over to a rock and sit down for a short rest.

Grant was visiting with Grandpa Conley at his beach house for the first time since his birth. Actually it was more than a visit, since his mother, Grandpa's daughter, Kate, had been admitted to the hospital and the doctors did not know what was wrong yet. Grant's father had asked his father-in-law to help by taking care of Grant until Kate was doing better.

Bob Conley and his wife Ruth lived a few blocks away from the ocean front in a small town on the coast. They had moved there years ago, before property values skyrocketed, and continued their modest lifestyle. They were retired and living on savings now. It was pleasant to have the ocean only a few minutes away by foot.

Grant was satisfied enough with his ceremonial foot-wetting on the first day, but the next day he wanted to go swimming. Bob was able to stall for another couple days while he looked into a swimming class. He was far too old to swim in the ocean himself, and could not by any means qualify as a life guard. So far they had been walking on a secluded beach down the street from Bob's house, which he preferred to the tourist area. To take the sting out of disallowing the boy to swim for the third day in a row, Bob bought a little colored bottle at a local shop and carefully placed a message inside. He stashed the bottle in his pocket before taking Grant out for their daily walk to the ocean.

"Did you ever hear about Puff the Magic Dragon?" asked Grandpa of Grant.

"No," said Grant. "Who's that?"

"There's a song about him. He lives by the sea, you know." This got Grant's attention.

"Does he live around here?" asked Grant with wider eyes.

"I don't rightly know," said Grandpa. "But I do know that dragons like caves, and there's a cave off that way." He pointed south.

Grant was riveted. "Have you been there, Grandpa?"

"Once long ago," he said. "But I didn't see a dragon. Still, you never can tell what you might find near a sea cave. There are always creatures of one sort or another. At least sand crabs. Would you like to find a sand crab?"

"I bet that magic dragon is there!" said Grant with total conviction. "Let's go, Grandpa. If you're not afraid."

"I think if you hold my hand, I'll be fine," said Grandpa.

Together they traveled over sand and rocks, through bush and grass, until they reached a tiny cove. Bob knew it well from his earlier days. He and Ruth had moved here not long after all the children had left home, and they'd had many a second-honeymoon adventure on the weekends during long walks. The cave was sheltered from most of the current by virtue of being in this little cove, with very little water reaching it even during high tide.

"Wow!" said Grant when he saw the mouth of the cave for the first time. He was distracted just long enough for Bob to slip the bottle out of his pocket and quietly into the low water of the cove. He could hardly contain himself for the next five minutes while Grant tentatively explored the first five feet of the cave.

"Can you tell if he's in there, Grandpa?" said Grant, finally.

"No, no, there's no telling a thing like that."

"Why don't you go in there and look, and I'll guard the cave from out here," suggested Grant, bravely.

"That's a good idea," said Grandpa, "but I'd need a flashlight and my exploring gear before I could do that. Not to mention my shield, helmet and sword, in case the dragon is hungry."

"Do dragons eat old people?" asked Grant.

"Maybe not. But it's always good to be prepared," advised Grandpa. "Maybe we should just leave a little message for him and see if he answers."

"Okay," said Grant. Grandpa walked around the little cove, hoping Grant would spot the floating bottle, which he did immediately.

"Grandpa! Look at that!" Grant didn't do much looking before he waded in and grabbed the tiny bottle. He could see there was a paper inside, so he lost no time in uncorking it. "Can you read this, Grandpa?"

Grandpa took out his glasses and studied the markings on the paper. "I don't recognize these letters. Maybe this is dragon language," he said.

"Really?" exclaimed Grant. "That's awesome!!" He took the paper from grandpa but quickly realized that it didn't do him any good if he couldn't decipher it. "How do we find out what it means?" he asked.

"Well ....," said Grandpa, "I have some books at home about decoding various languages. Perhaps we should take this home and hit the books."

"Okay," said Grant.

"It might be dragon language, or it might be some other kind of language."

"Like what?" asked Grant.

"Oh, I don't know. Mermaid, or warlock, or perhaps it was a Russian spy," said Grandpa.

"What's that?"

"I think we will find out soon. Come along with me. Grandma will want us to help with supper, but then you and I will shut ourselves in my library for a few hours and delve into these mysteries."

"Right," said Grant, and the two of them went back the way they had come.

This escapade afforded Grandpa several days of introducing Grant to the wonders of stories, folklore and research. In the hours he had to himself while Grandma took Grant to swimming class or the grocery store, Bob carefully made three different keys for interpreting the message and enlisted the help of the local librarian in getting them typed up, put in an official-looking binding and stored at the reference desk of the library.

When they had learned much but exhausted the resources of Grandpa's personal library without being able to interpret the message, Grant escorted Grandpa to the public library. At the front desk, Grant asked the librarian if she had any books on dragon language and stuff like that. She went through the whole routine of showing him how to look on the computer, checking the shelves, and then checking the "rare book stack." She came back with the books that Grandpa had secretly prepared: *The Language of Dragons*, *Remembering Atlantis* and *The Sirens of the Sea*.

"These are the only three books I have that might fill the bill," the librarian said earnestly as she handed them to Grant. He remembered to say thank you, and then he and Grandpa went home with their "borrowed" books.

"Now what do we do, Grandpa?" asked Grant.

"Now I need to take a nap after all that excitement, but you could get us a head start on the project, if you felt you were in the mood," Grandpa said.

"Yes, I am in the mood," said Grant.

"All right, then," said Grandpa, and he pulled up a chair for Grant at the kitchen table. "Sit here and spread these books out where you have plenty of light and lots of room. My desk is really too small for a project like this. You're going to need some paper, too. Run and ask Grandma for some shelf paper. Don't mess with little scraps on a project like this."

Grant prepared himself completely according to Grandpa's instructions, then looked very carefully through the rare books, looking for symbols that matched the symbols on the message. This gave Grandpa a good long nap of at least two hours, with only a couple dozen interruptions.

"I found one Grandpa! What should I do?"

"Write down the letters underneath it on the paper. Then look for the next one," Grandpa said patiently.

When Grant had finished laboriously copying the letters for every symbol in the message, he ran over to show Grandpa.

"Ah, very good. But have you looked at the other two books yet?" he asked.

"No. All the symbols were in this book. I found them all, Grandpa."

"That's very good. That means we have a good book, there. But what if mermaids and dragons use the same symbols? We don't know if a mermaid, or a dragon or someone from Atlantis wrote the message, do we?"

"No," said Grant. "But I think it was the dragon."

"A good researcher would check out all the books, so see if you can find the symbols in the other books." Grant was going to resume his search, but at that moment Grandma pointed out that his favorite cartoon show was due to start, so that delayed the project.

By the end of the next afternoon, Grandpa and Grant had deciphered the message in three different ways. To be more precise, the equivalent human words had been transcribed painstakingly by Grant, not without errors, during Grandpa's naps so that Grandpa wouldn't interfere. Nothing was more heartbreaking to Bob Conley than to see an overbearing adult correcting a child to pieces before he even had a chance to try. He kept himself out of the way to avoid any possibility.

Grant brought a scroll of tattered shelf paper over to Grandpa just before dinner and said, "I'm all done, Grandpa! What does it say?"

Grandpa put on his glasses and studied the paper. "Very interesting. I think it lost a little bit in the translation, so we'll have to work on figuring this out. Then decide which is the right language."

Grant looked disappointed. "You mean you still can't read it?"

"Let me explain something," said Grandpa as he stretched out his stiff shoulders. "Sometimes it takes *time* to get the exact meaning of something, or to find out all about something, and this is time well spent. Things don't always happen instantly in life, my boy. Did you know there are men who spend years and years digging up old stuff and studying it to find out about people who lived a long time ago? Sometimes they find old bones of dinosaurs, for instance, and they have to very carefully put all the pieces of bones together, and then maybe they can work out, *if they spend enough time at it*, what the animal looked like. Now this here, Grant, (and he indicated the shelf paper), is a message from ... well, we don't even know who it is from, or what language they were using. But we do want to find out the right answer about it, don't we?"

Grant nodded.

"Well, then, I think we should give it the proper respect and time. What do you think?"

Grant nodded.

"Very good, then. We'll take this to my study right after supper and, with all your good work on this project, we should be able to make some real headway. All right?"

Grant nodded, and then they turned on the before-supper cartoons. Grandpa liked them, too.

After supper the two men dug into their research with vigor. Grandpa got out his magnifying glass, and even his binoculars, just for effect. They got more shelf paper from Grandma and began sorting through the words in the mostly deciphered scroll. Grandpa found a few copy errors, and got Grant to re-copy them. Then it was time for bed.

"First thing in the morning, when we're fresh," said Grandpa, "we'll do our final interpretation."

After a special breakfast made by Grandma, consisting of blueberry waffles, ham, hash browns and hot chocolate, the men resumed their project.

Grandpa held up the scroll and cleared his throat. "Are you ready to hear the messages?" he asked Grant.

"Yes, Grandpa," said Grant.

"All right. Here's the first one, from the book *Sirens of the Sea:*

TELL SECRETS IN CAVE AND DISASTER AWAITS YOU

"Oh, my! You didn't tell any secrets in the cave the other day, did you?" asked Grandpa.

"No," said Grant. "What happens if you tell secrets?"

"It says here that *disaster awaits you*, which means something bad will happen to you."

"Ohhh!" said Grant.

Grandpa adjusted his glasses, checked something with his magnifying glass, and then continued on down the scroll. "From *Remembering Atlantis* we have

ASK IN CAVE AND ANSWER COMES NEXT DAWN

"Hmmm. I wonder who answers?"

"Who, Grandpa?" asked Grant.

"Well, it doesn't say here *who* answers your question, but just that if you ask in the cave, you will get an answer when the sun comes up the next morning."

"Wow!" said Grant.

"And here's the last possible meaning for our message, from *The Language of Dragons.*

NINE MINUTES IN CAVE AND MERMAIDS TAKE YOU

"Ah! We don't want that to happen, after those other stories we read about mermaids, do we?" said Grandpa.

"No!" said Grant.

Grandpa put the shelf paper scroll down, took off his glasses, put away the magnifying glass, and looked at Grant. "Well, what do you think?"

"About what?" asked Grant.

"Why, about our research," said Grandpa.

"Can I have some lemonade?" said Grant.

Grandpa tried to hide his disappointment by saying cheerfully, "Grandma probably has it all ready about now." Grant ran out of the study to check. Bob had been hoping that the final deciphering would have been more interesting to Grant, but you just never know what will capture the fancy of a child and what won't. He put away his binoculars and carefully rolled up the scroll and placed it in Grant's room.

The message in the bottle did, however, make an impression on Grant, even if not the way that Grandpa had expected. When Grant's mother was out of the hospital and doing better a few weeks later, he packed the little bottle with its message carefully in his suitcase, and left the shelf paper scroll behind. Somehow knowing the meaning of the message, even if it was only three possible meanings, was anti-climactic. On top of that, he couldn't read the scroll anyway, but he could admire the mysterious eight characters on the message in the bottle. He could dream that it meant anything he wanted, and that it was from a magic dragon.

Eleven years later Grant had occasion to stay with Grandpa again, while his parents were on a second honeymoon in Europe. That night after dinner, Grant brought out the bottle.

"Look, Grandpa! I still have this message from the dragon. I really believed it was from a dragon for a long time."

"Well, how 'bout that," chuckled Grandpa. "I still have the scroll we used to translate the message. I'll get it. I haven't thought of that for years."

Grant helped himself to a couple of sandwiches and a bowl of cereal while Grandpa rummaged through his shelves. He found the scroll at last and unrolled it for Grant, who looked at it with some amusement.

"That's my writing?" asked Grant. "I don't even remember doing that!"

"As I recall," said Grandpa, "the only thing you remembered after all that work was the next treat you wanted from Grandma's kitchen." Grandpa did all the cooking now, because Grandma had passed from this life about a year ago.

"Studying is not my strong point, Grandpa. I'm better at sports. Is there a basketball court around here? I can show you some of my cool stuff."

"I'm sure we can find one somewhere," replied Grandpa.

Grant read aloud from the scroll. "*Ask in cave and answer comes next dawn.* That's cool, grandpa! I should try that. Not that I believe in dragons or anything, but it would just be fun to try it. Where is this cave?"

Grandpa took him outside and pointed out the street that led to the beach, then gave him brief directions on getting to the cave. "But don't stay long, now. You know the mermaids will take you if you stay even nine minutes."

"Right, Grandpa!" said Grant as he ran off down the street.

Grandpa made some plans of his own, priding himself on how well he remembered being sixteen years old. He happened to have overheard Mrs. Steeley and Mrs. Fairwood talking the other day and knew just what to do.

Grant made his trip to the cave and was back in time for supper. Grandpa gave Grant some money for going out to the local movie theater after supper, and they went to bed shortly after he arrived home. "Tomorrow is the day the maid comes to do the housework, so we'll have to be up and out of here early. I just make a point of taking a long walk so she doesn't have my big feet in the way of everything she's trying to do."

The next morning, just before the sun rose, Grandpa was up puttering around in the kitchen, making a little breakfast for the two of them. "Time to get up, Grant," he said quietly into the spare bedroom. "You don't want the maid to see you in your underwear, do you?"

Grant mumbled something and pulled the covers over his head. Grandpa gave him a few more minutes and then brought the breakfast in to him in bed. "Aren't you expecting an answer at dawn?" he asked Grant.

That got Grant out from beneath the covers. "I forgot! Am I supposed to be at the cave for the answer?"

"Don't know," said Grandpa. "Wolf down a little bit of this breakfast as long as you're sitting up, and then maybe you ought to head out."

Grant finished the plate of scrambled eggs in four bites, grabbed the bacon and ate it on the way to the bathroom, and was dressed and ready to go out the door just as the doorbell rang.

"Oh, would you get that?" asked Grandpa. "Must be the maid."

Grant opened the door and on the doorstep stood the most beautiful girl he had ever seen. She had pale skin, big eyes and soft, curly brown hair. She smiled and said, "I'm supposed to do some cleaning for Mr. Conley."

"Oh!" said Grant. "Come in."

"Hello Misty," said Grandpa. "Thank you for being right on time. This is my grandson, Grant. Grant, this is Misty Fairwood."

"Hi Grant," said Misty, and every thought of dragons, bottles and caves went straight out of his head.

"Hi Misty," said Grant.

And the rest is folklore, as told by the many descendants of Misty and Grant.

THE FAIRY OF GRUENWALD HOUSE

By Colette Bree

"Fairy Ring!" Cassandra called, and one by one the Columbia River fairies flew over to join the circle.

"I prophesy," intoned Cassandra, "that our ways will change forever today, and that it will be a grievously hard year."

"Nonsense!" shouted several of the fairies. They never believed Cassandra's prophesies, even though they always came true, if anyone cared to notice.

The Fairy Ring descended upon the moss just as the first notes of Fairy Music sounded. Few humans have heard Fairy Music. It is not made with musical instruments but emanates when many fairies are gathered together with their attention upon their Queen. It is somewhat like the sound of a harp, but with a hint of the ping of a glockenspiel, tempered to imitate a human-but-almost-divine voice. Some of the more ethereal Celtic musicians have captured a sound that is almost like Fairy Music, which is most likely why they are so popular today.

Minerva glided into the Fairy Ring on a falcon and disembarked. She smiled and beckoned to them all to follow her on a tour of her entire Domain. She commended each fairy for her accomplishments of the year and pointed out their good works. "I would especially like to commend Penelope, Fairy of the Trees," she added. "Nowhere in the entire Kingdom of Earth are there lovelier trees." The other fairies hummed and nodded in agreement.

Instead of returning to their Gathering Place at the top of the Falls, Minerva swerved out the opposite direction and flew west until the fairies were hovering over the City, domain of People.

"It's been many years since we've gone among the People," said Minerva. "Hundreds of years ago they began ignoring us until most of them could no longer see or hear us."

"I knew some children for three summers," said Pomona wistfully. "I showed them where all the juiciest, ripest blueberries and blackberries were to be found. They brought them home to their mother for making pies. They told her about me, but she would not believe them. Finally on the fourth summer they came no more. Very sad."

"Yes," said Minerva. "But because of the chaos that is coming over land and sky from the cities of the people, it is my belief that we must make another try. And another. We must keep trying to work with the People before our own dominions are ruined forever. I believe it is our duty. We have a different magic from the People, and I believe they need our help."

The Fairy Music warbled and wavered in confusion as the fairies tried to understand Minerva's direction. "Therefore," stated Minerva, "I would like to grant each of you the domain of your heart's desire as usual; with one exception. I trust faithful Penelope to be the first to venture into new territory. Penelope is to be Fairy of Gruenwald House."

The Fairy Music ebbed to a low vibrato of astonishment and Minerva bid them follow her to the Gruenwald House. They hovered above the rooftop as she explained that it was a house full of normal People, and Penelope was to work such magic there as she could. At the next gathering she would teach her experiences and then other fairies would be assigned to the People.

"But I haven't the faintest idea what to do about People!" murmured Penelope, in shock. "Mightn't I just continue with the Trees, Queen Minerva? I know how to make their bark strong, how to help them reach for the sun and bring on their new buds and leaves. I know very much about trees, and hardly even know what a People is."

"There, there, dear," said Minerva gently. "I know it will be hard at first, but soon you will know the People as well as the Trees. I chose you especially because you are devoted and faithful. These are the qualities that I am sure will work magic in the Gruenwald House, Penelope. You will see. We leave you now, but at sunrise you will be the Fairy of Gruenwald House. I am sure you will not disappoint me."

Minerva turned her attention to the other fairies. "Wish her luck, my dears, and then we will be on our way."

Penelope watched them fly off and lighted in the grass by the house, mournfully. Just then the sun peeked over the horizon and she enjoyed her favorite moment of the day. She soared through the yard, whirring in and out of tree canopies and giving each tree a liberal sprinkling of fairy dust. Small wonder that passersby that day found the Gruenwald yard uncommonly beautiful.

Sounds began to issue from the Gruenwald house. Water ran in the pipes, the coffee grinder clamored, and rock and roll music blared from an upstairs bedroom. Penelope flew over to the kitchen window and watched Mrs. Gruenwald preparing breakfast. When the front door opened as Mrs. Gruenwald retrieved the morning paper, Penelope flew in after her. She was not noticed.

Mr. Gruenwald shuffled into the dining room and sat down. Mrs. Gruenwald set a plate of eggs before him and poured his coffee. Penelope alighted in the center of the table and introduced herself to Mr. Gruenwald very politely.

"Good day, Mr. Gruenwald," she said. "I am Penelope, your house fairy, sent by Queen Minerva of the Columbia River. How may I be of service to you?"

Mr. Gruenwald looked up with a most unusual expression on his face, then sneezed loudly. Penelope had to take flight to avoid being blown off the table. She flew back to her position and repeated her question, "How may I be of service to you?"

Mr. Gruenwald did not answer, did not even look up, but took a lengthy swig of coffee and grabbed the ketchup bottle.

"The least you could do is answer me!" said Penelope. She buzzed angrily in front of his face but he did not see her. He lifted the ketchup bottle and inverted it to swathe his eggs, but she zapped it with her wand saying, "Oh no you don't. If you won't listen to me then you won't have any of that, either."

Mr. Gruenwald shook and pounded on the bottle but could get no ketchup out of it. "Helen," he said testily, "This ketchup's no good. Won't come out of the bottle. Why do you always have to buy the cheap brand?"

"It's the brand *you* insisted I buy," Mrs. Gruenwald snapped as she took the bottle away. She ran hot water over it in the kitchen sink.

Mr. Gruenwald put on his glasses and attacked the newspaper while he was waiting for the ketchup. Penelope continued trying to get his attention, even throwing fairy dust at his glasses.

"I can't see a doggone thing!" he grumped, and took his glasses off to see what was wrong with them. Meanwhile Kelly Gruenwald came downstairs and bounced into the dining room.

"We have a field trip today, Dad. Guess where?" she chirped.

"Can't a man have peace and quiet in his own house?" Mr. Gruenwald roared.

"Sorry, dad," said Kelly quietly. She poured herself some cereal and began eating, spirits not dampened too badly.

Penelope hovered near Kelly and studied her. She threw a small bit of fairy dust towards Kelly. The girl looked up instantly and smiled brightly, then glanced sideways at her father to make sure he hadn't seen it. Penelope flew a few dainty little patterns in front of Kelly, and though Kelly paused and looked puzzled, she didn't focus on Penelope. But it was enough to give Penelope hope.

Penelope followed Kelly the whole day, observing silently. She noticed how much Kelly was cheered whenever she threw fairy dust on her. At the close of the day when Kelly was just ready to lay her head on her pillow, she said out loud, "I feel like I have a guardian angel. I've heard of them, and I don't mean to be rude, but I didn't really believe in them. Anyway, I think you're here now—my guardian angel, I mean—and I just want to say thank you, and that I'm glad you're here." She smiled.

Penelope zipped about the room with excitement and then hovered near Kelly's face, trying to place herself where Kelly's eyes focused, hoping that Kelly might be able to see her.

"I can't see you, but maybe I'm not supposed to," said Kelly.

"No, you *are* supposed to see me!" cried Penelope. "I'm right here! See?"

Kelly struggled as if she were trying to hear something. "I can't hear you either, though I seem to hear *something*.... but it might just be my imagination."

"No! It's not!" insisted Penelope. She threw some fairy dust toward Kelly.

Kelly smiled. "Oh well; whether you're just in my imagination or not, I think it will be great to have you around. But what is your name?"

"Penelope," the fairy answered.

"Oh," sighed Kelly. "I couldn't hear a thing. Should I call you Angel?" Penelope shook her head. "No, that's not right, is it? Well ... "

Kelly looked around the room and saw a penny lying on her dresser, which reminded her of the wish she'd made on a penny just last week at the wishing well at Grandma's house. She had wished for a special friend, someone who would *always* be her friend. "The penny wish!" she exclaimed. "It's come true! Do you mind if I call you Penny, then?" said Kelly to the air beside her.

Penelope flew to the spot that Kelly addressed and said, "Close enough; I'll take it!"

"This is good!" said Kelly. "Good night, Penny, and I don't know where you like to sleep, or if you sleep, but you're welcome to stay here, always." She whispered a fervently thankful prayer, then closed her eyes.

Penelope did not sleep, but she stayed until Kelly was asleep, then went out to be with the trees. Before daybreak, however, Penelope found a sprig of tiny blue flowers that had fallen and placed them over the penny on Kelly's dresser. Kelly arose shortly after her alarm went off, and when she was walking to her dresser to get her clothing she noticed the tiny flowers.

"Penny!" she gasped. She stood for a few moments, hushed with wonder, and finally said, "Thank you, Penny! They're beautiful!"

Penelope spent the next few days in complete happiness, following Kelly through every step of her life, giving her occasional small surprises, and continuing to talk to her, hoping that one day she would hear. Just as Penelope felt that she had mastered her dominion, Kelly brought up a new and puzzling subject.

"Penny," she said one evening close to bedtime, "I know you're my guardian angel and not my brother's, but I wonder if there's something you could do about him. Mom says he's suffering from the disease of turning into a man, and I don't know if she was kidding or what, but Eric is just not the same. He won't talk to me anymore, and I think some of his friends are weird. I'm so afraid that he will do something stupid like take drugs or get beat up. Do you think you could watch over him for a few days and ... you know, make sure he doesn't get in any trouble? Could you please do that?"

Penelope flew back and forth nervously. "I'll try," she said, "but I don't know anything about the disease of turning into a man. I hope I won't disappoint you!"

"I am so grateful, Penny!" said Kelly, sensing that Penny had agreed to the task. "Thank you. I wish I could see you, though. That would be so nice."

Kelly closed her eyes and lay her head on the pillow. "Maybe if I think of you with my eyes shut I will be able to see you better. At least I can imagine.... "

Penelope lighted very gently on Kelly's hand and waited to see what she would say next. "I'm right here!" she said to Kelly. "You *can* see me. Just open your eyes!"

"Do you have pretty blue wings, Penny?" asked Kelly. "That is how I picture you. And with golden hair. Am I right?"

"You *can* see me!" said Penelope, amazed. "How did you do that with your eyes shut?"

Kelly didn't say anything further because she had fallen fast asleep.

The next day Penelope held to her pledge and spent the day with Eric. He looked a fright when he walked out of his bedroom first thing in the morning, bags under his eyes, prickly hairs sprouting unevenly over the lower half of his face and the hair on the top of his head standing on end here and there. She threw a large dose of fairy dust at him straightaway. He took a deep breath and blinked his eyes, then continued toward the bathroom. She watched with fascination as he shaved and washed himself. The final result was such an improvement that she sprinkled him merrily with a double helping of fairy dust and was pleased to see that he did a little dance step and smiled at himself in the mirror. He walked jauntily out to the dining room, grabbed a piece of toast and his jacket, said

"Nice shirt, Kel" to his sister and sashayed to the front door.

Kelly beamed in the direction of Penelope, who was following Eric out the front door.

"Edward, did you hear that?" said Mrs. Gruenwald. "He actually complimented his sister! Maybe he's going to live through puberty after all."

Mr. Gruenwald continued to read his paper.

"Edward!"

"Oh—no dear, no more coffee for me, thank you," said Mr. Gruenwald.

Kelly and Mrs. Gruenwald rolled their eyes and smiled at each other.

Penelope managed to avert some close calls for Eric that day in school. On at least two occasions he was staring at a girl instead of paying attention in class. She pulled out the arrow that Diana had given her and jabbed him in the nose, which promptly brought his attention front and center. He brushed at his nose to see if a mosquito had bitten him.

"And what kind of curve do we have here?" the algebra teacher was asking, pointing to an equation on the board. "Eric?" she asked. Eric was about to make one of his usual flippant attestations to ignorance when Penelope threw fairy dust at him and drew a parabola in the air with her wand. He forgot what he had been going to say.

"Parabola! Parabola!" Penelope shouted at him.

"Crabola," said Eric absently, and the class burst into laughter so suddenly that it surprised him.

The teacher blushed slightly, aware that she had been a bit crabby lately. "Very witty," she said. "And does the parabola open up or down?" she queried.

Penelope flew back and forth between his ears as fast as she could, shouting "Down!" into each one.

"Down?" said Eric, rubbing his ears.

"That's right," said the teacher. She called on another student for the next question.

Eric sat puzzled in his chair, wondering how he had accidentally answered the questions correctly. It had been his policy to answer all questions with the most irritatingly inept answers. Teachers hated that because it proved they couldn't do their job, at least not with him. "Oh well," he thought, "at least it made the class laugh at Mrs. Chelsea."

After school Eric lingered in the back parking lot with some friends. He struck a match, getting ready to light up a cigarette.

"Oh no! Don't do that!" clucked Penelope. She blew the match out with a wave of her wand.

Eric pulled another match out of his matchbook and tried again to light his cigarette. The match went out again. A third match did the same. He threw the rest of the book down with disgust.

"Pick that up!" scolded Penelope. "Now you throw that right in the trash because you shouldn't be smoking. What kind of example does that set for those girls?" she hissed.

Eric looked over his shoulder and saw two very cute sophomore girls approaching. Penelope threw fairy dust their way and one came right up to Eric, picked up his matchbook and said, "Did you drop this?"

"Oh... " said Eric, thinking fast and stuffing the unlit cigarette discreetly into his back pocket. "I must have. Just some litter I found on the ground. Here, let me throw that away." He took it from her and pitched it neatly into the trash can on the sidewalk.

"Good shot!" exclaimed cute girl number two, smiling at him with such admiration that it gave him a funny feeling.

"You walking this way?" asked cute girl number one.

"As a matter of fact, I am," he said as he joined them, walking in the opposite direction from his home.

"You were so funny in algebra class today!" said the second girl.

"Oh, it was nothing," Eric said modestly.

"Maybe you can help us out with this homework assignment. I still can't figure out how to get these equations to come out," said the other girl.

"Sure," he volunteered. And though he nearly broke out into a cold sweat when he opened the algebra book at the table in the first girl's home, with her mother looking on, he found that one actually could pick up how to do the problems by following the examples. In fact, it was kind of fun. If he amazed the girls with his skill, he amazed himself even more. Who would have ever thought it?

Penelope spent the rest of the week with Eric, by which time three-fourths of the Gruenwald household was in glowing spirits. Penelope found that Mrs. Gruenwald thrived as long as her children were doing well and she could encourage them along with help, surprises and advice; she could see that she made a difference to them. "It's almost as if she's part fairy herself," thought Penelope. "Maybe she has some kind of dust or magic that I can't see."

Observing Mr. Gruenwald filled her with skepticism, however. Penelope had been holding a grudge against him since her first day, but she now faced the fact that he was undoing part of her good work every day with his ill-humored remarks and demands. Something would have to be done about him.

"Who took the TV guide!?" he roared that evening from his favorite chair.

"I think you're sitting on it, dad," said Kelly from the couch.

"Your thief of a brother probably left it in his room again. Run up and get it."

"I'll look, but I don't really think—"

"We don't have time for you to think! Get up there before the 9:00 show starts," he barked.

Kelly sighed and ran up the stairs, but Helen said, "I thought you had to work on some reports tonight, dear."

"I'm going to do them after I relax a bit, and I certainly don't need any of your nagging. I've told you and told you that I need peace and quiet after a long day of work, and what do you do? You carp at me from the minute I walk into the door."

Mrs. Gruenwald was unfazed. "I didn't mean to nag you," she said quietly, "but I know that I will be the one to blame if you fall asleep watching TV and the reports don't get done."

"I can't find it in Eric's room, dad," said Kelly, bounding down the stairs. She went over and grasped his hairy arm. "I'll make you some nachos if you'll just stand up a minute so I can see if you're sitting on it."

"Get out of here," he said with venom.

"Come on dad," Kelly urged, pulling slightly on his arm.

"I'm going to dock your allowance." He heaved himself up out of the chair with Kelly's help and Kelly picked up the crumpled TV guide from the seat of the chair.

"Here, dad." Kelly handed him the TV guide.

"It wasn't there when I sat down," he grumbled. "And why aren't those nachos done yet?"

Penelope watched all this from her favorite spot on the mantle, next to a cuckoo clock. "Such a nasty temper I have never seen!" she exclaimed in spite of herself. Kelly looked right at her and smiled. "All right, Kelly. Here goes!" said Penelope.

She flew over to Mr. Gruenwald's chair and hovered for a moment while Kelly tiptoed quietly upstairs. Mrs. Gruenwald had retired to the sewing room to work on a quilt, and Eric was still at the library doing research for a term paper.

Penelope swirled around and around Mr. Gruenwald, giving him light sprinklings of fairy dust, but his only apparent response was to the TV.

"Helen, where's my remote!? I *hate* this commercial! Where is it? Helen!" He had thrown the TV guide and a couple other magazines at the TV before Helen came to the rescue. He muted the sound and then promptly fell asleep before his show came on. Within minutes his snoring was ear-splitting, while the 9:00 show flashed soundlessly before him on the TV.

Penelope flew up to the lamp above the end table next to Mr. Gruenwald's chair. "What a strange creature you are!" she said to his sleeping form.

"Mind your own business!" said an ugly, caustic voice.

"Who said that?" said Penelope. Mr. Gruenwald was still sleeping.

"You're one to talk about being strange," the voice continued, "when you look like a mutant insect."

Penelope strained to see who was speaking and finally spotted a small, furry thing with bloodshot eyes and skinny, claw-like hands peeking out from underneath Mr. Gruenwald's jowl.

"What in the name of Minerva...?" she uttered in astonishment.

"I'll thank you to leave Ed here alone in the future. You've put him to sleep with all that filthy residue you put all over him."

"What?" cried Penelope. "I didn't put any filthy—are you talking about my fairy dust?"

"If that's the lame name you've given it. Get that stuff off of my man right now! This place is too, too quiet and we've got to stir up some trouble before these other humans get anything done around here. I'm in the mood for fighting!"

"I am *not* going to remove my fairy dust," said Penelope indignantly. "Minerva sent me here to help these People. And what, might I ask, are you doing here?"

"So you think you're a fairy, do you? Everyone knows there is no such thing. Get lost."

"Well, *everyone* seems to be wrong because I do exist," said Penelope.

"People believe anything we tell 'em, and therefore you do not exist. Ha!" The creature cackled gleefully. He laughed so hard he lost his grip and tumbled down to Mr. Gruenwald's chest, where he latched on with his claws and began his ascent back up to Mr. Gruenwald's neck.

Penelope watched and slowly realized that she was looking at a demon. She'd run across them occasionally in the forest, but none this obnoxious and ugly. One good thing about demons was that they were very stupid, which made it easy to get rid of them.

"I suppose you're here because you're too weak to deal with the really influential People, eh?" said Penelope.

"Liar!" spat the demon.

"Only fairies know where to find the People who control the big weapons that can destroy the Earth."

"Impossible!" said the demon. "

If you don't believe me then I suppose I shall have to go visit them by myself," said Penelope, and she began to fly off.

"No!" shouted the demon. "You're taking me with you. If you don't, I will make his nose turn black and fall off!" The demon latched onto Mr. Gruenwald's nose, pretending he could carry out his threat at any moment.

"Oh dear, no!" cried Penelope in mock distress. "I can't let you do that! All right, I will just have to take you with me. She waved her wand and the demon was encased in a little traveling harness with a two-foot leader. Penelope fastened the leader to her ankle.

"Let go now," she said to the demon as she started to fly. He released his hold on Mr. Gruenwald somewhat grudgingly, after a few seconds of tugging from Penelope. Demons were rather stubborn in this way, as they had no real means of locomotion themselves and their entire purpose was to latch onto to some other vital life form and wreak havoc with it.

Penelope flew the demon out the chimney and across the city until she was in her own familiar forest territory. She found the largest boulder she could, landed the demon on it and released the harness. She had mercifully placed him on a rather flat-topped boulder so that he wouldn't have to struggle to hang on, but she knew he would still be quite distressed without any means of escape and no life form to heckle. She flew away quickly, ignoring his blood-curdling squalls of protest.

Back in the Gruenwald house, she alighted on the arm of Mr. Gruenwald's chair and watched. He woke up from his nap, looked at the time, then rose and turned off the TV. He sat down in his chair again, but this time he had his briefcase and opened it up on his lap.

Penelope noticed that Kelly had come out of her room and was standing silently on the stairwell, almost out of sight, peering down at her father. Penelope did a somersault as she cast fairy dust all around Mr. Gruenwald. When Penelope looked up at the stairs again, Kelly's eyes were wide and her hand was over her mouth.

"Can she see me?" wondered Penelope.

Penelope flew up the staircase until she was hovering three feet in front of Kelly. Kelly slowly lowered her hand from her mouth. "I must be imagining this," she murmured. She held out her hand as if to invite Penelope to light on it. Penelope did.

Kelly brightened as she felt the feathery touch of Penelope's slippers on her hand.

"You're a *fairy*!" whispered Kelly.

Penelope curtseyed. "I am Penelope, your house fairy, sent by Queen Minerva of the Columbia River. How may I be of service to you?"

That is how humans became reacquainted with fairies. Has it happened yet in your house?

A Primrose in the Morning

By Colette Bree

On a cold and windy Saturday morning, when the dew was still out, Darcy Mendelssohn decided to take a walk. Normally she wouldn't be caught dead out in the weather, as she had very delicate health, but something in her made this daring decision anyway.

"Get out of my way, Wilfred," she said brazenly to her cat. Wilfred was far too fat, and he stood blocking her path in the doorway, waiting to be petted and fussed over. "You're just a big, gray blotch of fur and you're not going to stop me from this adventure."

Wilfred meowed sarcastically as if to say, "What adventure? Getting your feet wet?"

Darcy picked him up and ruffled his fur roughly. "Just because you like nothing better than to sleep on a soft blanket all day doesn't mean that the rest of us are that lazy. You old fleabag!" She tossed him into the nearest chair, which caused him to protest loudly. Darcy then ran out the door, letting the screen door bang behind her. Normally she was very careful about the screen door as she hated the racket it made, but today she didn't mind.

The leaves had been falling for a number of days now, and the streets and sidewalks were littered with them. She'd not been walking long when a pure white cat ran across her path and stopped to look back at her.

"Ho! Who are you? I've never seen you in this neighborhood," she said to the cat.

The cat answered by running further up the sidewalk and around several trees, then pausing again.

"I suppose you think I ought to follow you. Is that what you want? Why don't you let me pet you? Here kitty, kitty." Darcy held out her hand to beckon the cat.

The cat watched noiselessly as Darcy approached slowly, then ran off again. "Aren't you the tease!" exclaimed Darcy. "I don't *have* to pet you, you know. I was offering it for your enjoyment. The least you could do is hold still a moment." Darcy resumed walking before she had finished scolding the white cat, and began to grow curious. She did not know, as most of you probably do, that curiosity can be the most wonderful and dangerous thing.

The cat continued to run in fits and spurts, always stopping to look back at Darcy before disappearing completely from sight. Darcy had walked three miles before she knew it, and was on the edge of a small wooded park that sloped down into a ravine. The cat ran through the leaves that had been heaped up over the last week.

"My ankles are getting wet!" exclaimed Darcy to the cat, as she waded through the dewy leaves, which dampened her socks. She continued following the cat, nevertheless. She had not dressed properly for such an outdoorsy activity, since she had done it on quite a spur-of-the-moment impulse.

As the cat navigated through gnarled and naked trees, Darcy became aware that they were headed straight into the ravine. "Hey, where are you taking us!?" she protested to the cat. The cat ignored her and continued steadily downward.

At last they reached a small depression, surrounded by a surprisingly even circle of trees. The tree on the highest piece of ground was relatively free of leaves at its base, presumably because they had tumbled downward into the depression as winds swept through the park and down the ravine. Just at the base of the tree there were a few flowers. Darcy watched the cat very deliberately take a seat near the flowers and begin purring.

"So you're a flower-loving cat, are you?" said Darcy, finally getting within petting distance of the white cat. The cat allowed Darcy to pet it at last.

"Good kitty," said Darcy as she stroked the cat's smooth, white fur. "I am so tempted to pick a flower!" she exclaimed to the cat, "but I know I'm not supposed to do that."

The cat meowed as if to say, "Pick one, and hurry up about it," and then nudged her hand toward the flower.

"Well, I suppose it wouldn't hurt to pick just one," said Darcy, "as there are at least several others here. I haven't a clue what kind of flower would be blooming out here in the middle of a leafy wood on such a cold morning." She picked a flower, delicately, and then lifted it to her face to see if it had a fragrance. "No smell, but it's pretty just the same," said Darcy to the cat, who watched her attentively. "Here, check it out." She lowered the flower to the cat, who sniffed it with great interest for a very long time.

Darcy began laughing, partly because the sight of a cat sniffing a flower was amusing, but also because she was feeling a little light-headed. She laughed and laughed, until the whole world seemed to be getting light and blurry ....

"All right, all right," the cat was saying to her. "It can't be that funny. Let's just gather ourselves together now."

Darcy wiped her eyes, which had been full of tears from all her laughing, and opened them wide in disbelief when she saw the white cat standing upright before her, speaking to her as he held the flower. Darcy presumed it was a he-cat, at any rate, as the voice was deep and masculine.

They were no longer in a wood. The cat was wearing a space helmet with a purple collar, and a Fleet Cat emblem on his breast. They were standing near a waist-high planter of flowers. A butterfly flitted over and landed upon the cat's fingertip when he offered it.

"Hello, Ralphie," said the cat.

"Hello," said the butterfly. "Just flying through. I'm on my way to the bazaar. Are you going?"

"I don't think so," said the cat. "I have a guest." The cat indicated Darcy. "Ralphie, I'd like you to meet Darcy, from Earth. Darcy, this is Ralphie, originally of Seconda in the Paloose System. He is now a citizen of our Primrose Planet."

"Pleased to meet you," said Darcy, wondering why she did not feel more rattled. "And your name?" she asked the Cat.

"Oh, I *am* sorry," he said. "I completely forgot that you don't speak the cat language on Earth. I did tell you my name was M'Zeetfir, but you probably didn't understand a word of what I was saying. You did follow me, though, all the way to our beautiful Primrose Planet, and that is extraordinary."

"Funny," said Darcy. "I don't even remember getting on a space ship."

"Wasn't necessary," said M'Zeetfir. "The primrose patch I showed you is a portal. You were teleported."

"Sounds like science fiction or something," said Darcy. "I've never had an adventure like this before. Maybe I'm still in bed dreaming, and didn't really wake up and go on a walk."

"Oh no," said M'Zeetfir. "This is quite real. Let me explain. The Primrose Planet is a vacation planet. In busy galaxies where the folks work long and hard to keep the good games of life going, they appreciate a place like this."

"It is pretty, I will admit," said Darcy. "But what's so special? I mean, I see lots of nice scenery, but I don't see any malls, or skyscrapers, or even much traffic. Looks just like a small Earth city. Well, it does look a lot cleaner, I will say, and it does seem very orderly. Probably don't have many policemen here, do you?"

"No, there's no need for that," said M'Zeetfir. "We choose our clients carefully. But let me tell you the special thing about the Primrose Planet. This Planet was developed by a genius named Alastair Jaquaramonde. He made use of the often-forgotten idea that time is really just a consideration that we citizens of the universe have agreed upon in order to keep everything neat and tidy. Mr. Jaquaramonde gathered a great many high-minded beings together and had them agree upon a different universe that contained a Primrose Planet, and that universe exists outside the normal agreements of time. Each of the known planets in civilized sectors have numerous portals to the Primrose Planet. While you are on the Primrose Planet, you are in effect "between" moments of time as you know it. When you go back through the portal to your home planet, no time will have passed at all! This makes it the ideal vacation planet, as those who deserve vacations the most are without fail the ones who cannot afford to take vacations and who are usually unwilling to take vacations because too many important operations would fall apart without them."

"Amazing!" said Darcy for lack of anything else to say.

"It was a brilliant idea," continued M'Zeetfir. "It's still fairly new, but soon enough we will see the end of burnout and nervous exhaustion. We've learned quite a bit already—and some of it unexpected. We consider that if we continue finding those individuals who most unselfishly give of their time and energies to make their worlds better, and we prop them up with a Primrose Planet vacation whenever needed, we will soon have a great number of very nice galaxies to live in.

"You know, the problem with most of the planets out there is that they are very wearing on a person. Life there is too hard, and not at all the fun thing it was intended to be. A person who tries to do anything about it often gets attacked instead of thanked, using the poorest excuses for reasoning imaginable.

"Then there are the regular, everyday people who are called upon to be heroes in miniature: the young son or daughter who must help a single parent raise the other children, the new mother and father who must help a struggling baby around the clock, the Florence Nightingales who pit themselves against a nearly unmoving and unfeeling bureaucracy to try to better conditions for the *less important* people."

"Cool idea," said Darcy, aware that she was taking the whole thing too much in stride. "But why did you bring me here? I'm no Florence Nightingale."

"To tell you the truth," said M'Zeetfir, "it was really just a spur-of-the-moment thing."

"Funny you should say that," exclaimed Darcy, "because it was for me, too. I never take walks, but suddenly I just had to take one."

"I had just finished setting up the first portal on Earth, and I wanted to test it," explained M'Zeetfir. "Earth as a whole is not quite ready to join us in this endeavor. Most heads of government don't even publicly acknowledge the existence of other life in the universe. But we were willing to give it a try anyway. I think that to succeed on Earth it would have to be the best keep secret on the planet."

"That's for sure," said Darcy. "I know guys who would take it over and charge people a lot of money for it. That's generally what they do on Earth, you know."

"So true," sighed M'Zeetfir. "And yet in all fairness we should remember that there are individuals and groups who devote lives to bettering the welfare of others, without demanding personal wealth in return."

"That's good to know. I think I've heard of some of those groups. I do have a question, though," said Darcy. "I was wondering how to get back home—I mean, I do rather like it here, and I do feel much more well than I ever felt at home, but just the same I was wondering how, just in case."

"Same way you got here, Darcy," said M'Zeetfir, "but I hope you will stay a while and take advantage of your vacation. Your students will be helped even more by you if—"

"How do you know I have students?" exclaimed Darcy. "For that matter, how did you know my name? And why did you ask me to follow you?"

"I have my sources," replied M'Zeetfir. "It's not exactly classified information. I happen to know that you are considered the best English-As-A-Second-Language teacher throughout the whole Russian community in your part of the state. People travel across the state or even from other states to stay with relatives in your area in order to take your course. And they build themselves new lives with what you teach them."

"They do?" she said, aghast. "I do try to do a good job, but I thought I was really an average teacher. And so much of the time I feel awful, with headaches or backaches or indigestion."

"The difference between you and other teachers, Darcy, is that you are not just going through the minimum number of motions required in order to collect a paycheck. It really matters to you whether the students learn how to speak English and get all their questions answered. You have a willingness to help that makes it very easy for them to learn. It is almost as magical as the portal to Primrose Planet."

That made Darcy smile. "And my family told me I was impractical to major in Russian! I've believed them all these years because I never have had a very high-paying job, but I have noticed that I get good recommendations from my students. Say, my headache just went away! This is wonderful!"

"That's the thing about the Primrose Planet," said M'Zeetfir. "The people who populate this planet seem to have a marked absence of the things that cause aches and pains. Their personal problems, turmoil, confusion and pain seem to melt away when out of the *contamination* of their home planets. Refreshed, they return to their everyday lives with even more energy to face the things that have been weighing them down."

Darcy resolved right then and there to return often to the Primrose Planet. She spent several days getting acquainted with the place and met a number of other Fleet Cats who took care of business on the planet, as well as other vacationers in all sorts of forms. Each day she felt brighter, more certain of herself and how she would conduct her life upon return to Earth, free of pain and illness. She began to discuss a plan with M'Zeetfir.

Exactly two weeks and one half day after she had arrived on the Primrose Planet, Darcy felt so strongly about what she wanted to do that she promptly went to the portal and returned to Earth. It did not take her long to find out about one of the organizations that M'Zeetfir had mentioned—one that is devoted to the bettering the lives of everyone on earth. She joined up right away.

Two weeks later, in her new uniform, she shared the secret of the Primrose Planet with her fellow staff members, according to M'Zeetfir's instructions. New portals were opened around the planet, and the secret was shared with other individuals and organizations who were helping create a new civilization on badly ravaged planet Earth.

So don't be surprised if you see some of the dire predictions for the next Millennium fail, and a new Golden Age emerges instead, for that will surely happen if those who care about Earth are helped to succeed.

A Frightful Halloween

By Colette Bree

"For cryin' out loud, will you get yourself in gear and find your hat? Edgar! What are you doing?"

Edgar quickly placed the cigar into his pocket, having enjoyed its fragrance for a fleeting moment. He placed the very forbidden box of cigars back behind the boxes on the closet shelf where he hid it from Alma.

"I'll be right there; just brushing the dust off my hat. Don't you ever clean in here?" he said loudly.

"No, I'm too busy cleaning up after you," she snapped, from so close behind him that he jumped. "Come on now or we'll be late."

"You're blocking my way," he said crossly.

She grunted and turned around, heading for the door. A few minutes later they were on their way to bingo. At least he hadn't let her talk him out of driving, though she was working hard at it. If she had to be the one behind the wheel and *he* was the back seat driver, *he'd* see all her mistakes too. What if he wasn't quite as sharp as he used to be? He still got them from here to there with no mishaps.

Edgar loved driving his Malibu. Even to take Alma to bingo. He didn't give a hoot about the bingo games, but he always went because it was his chance to excuse himself a couple times to use the restroom and sneak a few minutes with his cigar in the parking lot. The breeze wafted most of the evidence out of his clothing, and what was left he could blame on the other smokers in the huge bingo room. Yes, there were times he was thankful for the illogical thinking of women. Alma had made him promise to quit smoking years ago, but she never thought twice about dragging them both into the smoke-filled bingo den. The dad-blamed busybodies about town, however, were trying to pass a law to get rid of public smoking. Then he might have to think of a new way to sneak his cigars.

"Edgar," said Alma, interrupting his thoughts, "I've been thinking of skipping the Halloween business this year. It's so much trouble, and prices have gone up so much that I really don't think we should be buying all that candy and spending so much on decorations. Besides, we've got that Christmas trip to think about. You know my sister's grandchildren will be expecting presents."

Edgar's gut instinct told him to assert loudly and obnoxiously that she was *not* going to put a damper on his favorite holiday of the year. He knew, however, that it would never work with Alma. Thirty-five years of marriage and many painful mistakes had taught him that one doesn't enter into a dispute with Alma over anything one wishes to make happen. He had her completely figured out and she could be summed up in one word: *contrary*. A good way to get out of something he didn't really want to do was to insist to her that it was very important for him to do it. And people thought women were hard to understand! It had taken him eight years to prove it to himself, but he had found that without fail she would find a way to stop anything that he cared about doing.

"Well now you've got a point, Alma. The kids in this neighborhood don't respect us. They just think we're nice old people that give them treats. Time we quit being the nice guys."

"What are you talking about?" Alma said. "Of course we're nice. But we have to pinch our pennies, that's all."

"You're right!" he declared. "What do you say we go home right now and work out a new budget. I'm willing to give up bingo if you are, and then we can plan a big Christmas for your sister's grandkids. Take 'em to Disney World or something. It's time we quit spending money on the brats in our neighborhood and spent our money on family. What

GHOST
PARTY
B.y.O.
Booooos

do you say?"

"Oh, Edgar... I'm not sure about that. After all, Ellie's grandchildren have never even so much as written us a thank you note for any of the presents we've given them. To tell you the truth, I think they're spoiled."

"Alma, let's do it! We've had more than our share of bingo games. It would do me so much good to make those kids happy at Christmas. You know I'd spoil our own rotten if we had any."

"Edgar, I've told you not to bring up that subject with me," she answered ominously. She had been crestfallen at being childless.

"Sorry, dear. I just thought—"

"I don't see why we should change everything just because we're going to Cincinnati for Christmas. After all, we have our own lives and we have a place in the neighborhood. The children here are quite nice and they would be disappointed if we didn't have a Halloween show for them. You know that. No, we're not going to change anything. I've decided. You will dress up as usual. I will not allow you to ruin our good will in this neighborhood."

Edgar sighed his best sigh of resignation and said, "Oh, all right. It was just an idea."

"Edgar, you know very well that your ideas are always impractical," said Alma. "You should leave the ideas to me."

"I guess I should," he said. Inwardly he was elated and daydreamed of how much fun he would have next Saturday when the trick-or-treaters began knocking on the door. Unbeknownst to Alma he had already purchased his costume and all the props from his secret Halloween fund weeks ago. He loved kids, and Halloween was the perfect holiday as far as he was concerned because kids would come from near and far to knock on his door. He had the scariest place around that was free of charge, and he gave the best treats. With no children of his own to raise and educate, he'd easily saved enough money to retire last year, in spite of his big splurge every year on Halloween. Alma wouldn't let him be a scout master or other volunteer because she always felt he was "needed at home." So he had thrown all of his energies into Halloween for the past many years. Alma would probably go into cardiac arrest if she knew how much he really spent, but he managed somehow to keep it a secret.

Alma was freshening up her lipstick and didn't notice that they were approaching a red traffic light at forty miles per hour. They sailed into the intersection just as Gary Roth entered the intersection on a green light, driving a semi. He was going about two miles over the speed limit—fifty-two miles per hour. He was wide awake. Due to buildings and trees on the corner, he didn't see the Malibu until he was almost entering the intersection. He slammed on the brakes but didn't have time to hear the squeal of rubber on asphalt before the impact occurred.

The little Malibu crumpled on the passenger side, shattered glass exploded in the intersection and the Malibu went spinning diagonally out of the intersection and into an old brick building on the opposite corner. The impact loosened several tons of decorative brickwork and it fell onto the roof of the Malibu.

"I hate emergency duty!" said the angel, hovering nearby. Why do these gruesome accidents always happen on *my* watch?" He flew down and pulled Edgar and Alma out of the car and brought them up to his watch station, a few hundred yards above the intersection.

"Edgar, what was that?" asked Alma. "Has there been an accident? Why can't I see anything?"

"Don't know. I'm feeling a bit light-headed myself," he answered.

"Let me introduce myself," said the angel. "My name is Ben—short for Benedictus—and I will be your guide to the Pearly Gates."

"I think you need a guide yourself; to an asylum," said Alma to the man addressing her. He looked like he was wearing a monk's robe. "This is no time to be joking, young man. I think there's been an accident and someone ought to call an ambulance."

"Oh, the ambulance has been called," said Ben. "Hear it?" A siren blared below. "You're quite dead, though. Not a thing they can do for you. That's why I brought you up here."

Alma snorted but Edgar's eyes widened. He looked around and saw nothing but clouds. He looked down and saw the intersection below. Traffic was jammed and people were crowding around the building on the corner. A policeman had arrived and was setting out flares. Finally he saw his Malibu, crushed and battered almost beyond recognition against the side of the building.

"Alma, look down there," he said, pointing.

She looked below and it silenced her for a moment. "Edgar, this must be some kind of trick. Did you put something in my coffee? Maybe it's that new medication the doctor gave me last week. He said there were some side effects."

"No, Mrs. Gaston," said Ben. "You have passed out of your earthly existence. I know it is a bit disorienting, but that's why I'm here to make sure you reach the next destination. There is some reckoning to be done and so forth. You went to Sunday School so you know what I'm talking about."

"Yes, I know they taught something like that, but that was just to make the children behave. No one really *believes* it."

"They don't?" said Ben, mildly surprised. "Well, I admit the facts aren't *quite* straight in Sunday School—human error, you know—but I assure you that there's something up there for you, so let's be moving along, please."

"Edgar, please wake me up!" howled Alma to her husband. "I must be dreaming."

"No, dear," said Edgar. "I think he's right." He sighed. "I just wish I hadn't kicked the bucket until after Halloween. Isn't there some way I could just go back for a few days, Ben? The kids are counting on me."

"You should have thought of that," replied Ben, "when you cheated on the vision test at the DMV."

"I knew it!" cried Alma. "I told you I thought they were crazy to let you drive. Now look what you've done!"

"He was, after all, driving you to the bingo game at your insistence," reminded Ben.

Alma was silent. "So we're really dead, then," she said. "Just like that?

"It's that simple," said Ben. "If you will please follow me, now, we'll go on up and I'll show you your next step."

"Wait a minute," said Edgar. "If I'm not mistaken, aren't there special cases where the *departed* can stay on earth for a while to handle loose ends, or haunt castles, or whatever?"

Ben smiled. "Stories do get around, don't they? I don't recommend the practice myself. It's much more efficient to simply get on with your next step. So, let's proceed—"

"No," said Edgar. "I'm not going."

"You have to understand something about Edgar," said Alma to the angel. "He can't seem to get anything right the first time. He can't even get being *dead* right. There's no reasoning with him, either. I've found that out the hard way. You just have to either let him make his mistake or drag him along under protest. Take your pick."

"Thank you for your views," said Ben, "but I'm really not authorized to do any arguing on this matter. Oh dear, I've got another emergency so I've got to run. I will give you until October 31st at midnight to remain down here, and then I'll take you up with me. Enjoy your costume change."

"Please reconsider! Don't leave me here with this man!" cried Alma as the angel flew off.

"*You're* the one who married him," said the angel. "I'm sure you can last a few more days." Then he was gone.

"This is perfectly frightful, Edgar! What have you done? What were you-- EEEEEEAAAHHGGHH!" she screamed.

"What's the matter now?" said Edgar.

"You scared me," she said. "You're a ghost!"

Edgar turned to look at her. "How about that! So are you. This is great! I've never had a costume that came close to this." Edgar admired his spooky, wraith-like form.

"Edgar, *you* may like being a ghost, but I am mortified. I want you to get us out of this mess right now."

"You heard the guy, Alma. He's coming back to get us on the 31st. That's four and a half days from now. We've got a lot of work to do before then. I have to find someone to run my Halloween Show, and if you don't get down to the bingo game you'll never know who wins the jackpot."

"As if I care who wins the jackpot now," she said sourly. "I'm going with you."

"Suit yourself," he said.

They found they could quickly fly wherever they wanted to go, so Edgar headed for Tim Baker's house and Alma followed. Tim was a retiree who lived down the street from the Gastons. He was watching a ball game on TV and sipping on a beer.

"Hey Tim, you'll never guess what happened!" said Edgar as they landed near him. Tim continued watching the game as if nothing had happened. Edgar flew around and around him, entreating him to answer. There was no sign that Tim perceived him in the slightest.

"A fat lot of good this is doing us!" said Alma. "We've got four days to be ghosts and say good-bye to all these people we know who don't believe in ghosts. Does that make sense?"

"I thought Tim believed in the hereafter," said Edgar, puzzled.

"This is just too Wizard-of-Oz-y, Edgar," said Alma. "We probably just got a good crack on the head and we're dreaming all of this."

"Both of us, huh?" said Edgar.

"I don't know what *you're* doing, but I know *I'm* dreaming," said Alma. "And I can't wait to wake up."

"If you're just dreaming, then, why don't you do something totally dream-like and be quiet for a few minutes?"

"That'll be enough of your wise cracks," said Alma.

"What's the difference? It's only a dream."

Alma sighed. "I know, I know. I'm just following you, waiting to wake up."

They traveled around to all of their family members, trying to communicate to them. By the next day they found some of them involved in making arrangements for the funeral or execution of the will.

"Do you still think you're dreaming?" asked Edgar.

"Of course," said Alma. "This couldn't possibly be real. No one's even grieving over our death."

"Maybe they're not sorry we're dead. We've only visited *your* family so far."

"Edgar! Don't talk that way!"

"Sorry," he said.

"They flew back to their old house and found a group of school children gathering on the sidewalk, looking sad. Several of the girls were crying. Alma tried to comfort them but they didn't take any notice of her at all.

"Makes me feel like a real dolt," mumbled Edgar quietly. "Oh well.... too late now."

They flew all the way out to Florida to find Edgar's mother after that. She was just getting ready to go to the airport to fly out for the funeral. They accompanied her on the airplane. Edgar noticed that if he spoke soothingly to her she would stop her crying.

Alma was spellbound at the funeral. "Edgar! Who's paying for all this?" she gasped. "It's the loveliest funeral I've ever seen."

"I paid for it," he said proudly. "Took care of that long ago. I thought we should go out in style and not be a burden to our survivors."

"How dare you spend all that money without consulting me!" she flared, but then added, "It *was* very thoughtful of you, though. Thank you."

"Now do you think you're dreaming?" he asked.

"I'm *sure* I'm dreaming," she asserted. "The Edgar I know would *never* have paid for a funeral in advance. Especially one this nice."

Edgar sighed.

Halloween night came and Edgar hadn't managed to contact anyone about conducting his Halloween spectacle for the children, so he decided he would have to put it on himself. As a ghost he found himself not only unable to get anything communicated to humans, but also incapable of moving objects around with his appendages as he was used to doing. He tried "mind power" and that didn't work either. All he seemed to be able to do was fly around from here to there and talk with Alma. He was hoping that Halloween would somehow make things different.

Twilight came and the first trick-or-treaters appeared on the street. Edgar saw a boy dressed as a ghost walking up to a house with his bag. "Look Alma! There's a ghost. Let's try him first."

"You know darn well he won't even notice us," she said, but she followed him.

Edgar flew spirals around him, using the word "boo" liberally. The boy stopped in his tracks for a moment.

"Edgar, there's a white cat looking at you!" said Alma, laughing. There were several small white cats in the yard, all very curious about the ghosts.

"Well I'll be...." murmured Edgar. "Mrs. Lamont's white kitties are the first creatures we've run across that can see ghosts. Cute little things, aren't they?"

A sinister cackling issued from the porch of the house and a figure in swishing black skirts jumped into motion.

"What are you waiting for?" it said in a scratchy voice. "Come here, my pretty, and have some nice caaaaandy…" The witch extended its arm and the trick-or-treater advanced.

"Mrs. Lamont!" exclaimed Edgar. "Who would've thought. I didn't know she had it in her! She likes those kids, though. She must have thrown this together in the last couple days." They watched as the trick-or-treater braved spider webs, chilling music, hoots and howls and jumping things in the dark in order to get his treat. When he finally got it, he went running down the street to tell his friends, and soon whole troops were approaching the Lamonts' place.

"It's good to know the kids got their Halloween," said Edgar. "And I'd like to point out that you haven't woken up yet."

"Don't worry. I will," said Alma.

"While you're waiting, then, how about if we check out all the other haunts in the city? We've always stayed home on Halloween. I'm just curious."

"I don't care," said Alma.

They flew off and visited various "haunted houses," Halloween parties and bands of trick-or-treaters about the city. As midnight approached, Edgar bragged to Alma that he was sure he had made goose bumps appear on more than one neck.

"So what?" she said. "You probably went through at the same time as a breeze."

"No, I'm sure it was me. I think I'm getting the hang of it."

"It's time for us to go back to where we met that fellow in the robe," said Alma.

"I'm not going, and I don't think you should, either. It's just a dream, after all. What does it matter if you don't do what that fellow says?"

"It certainly hasn't gotten me anywhere following you," she said.

"How can you say that? I thought you were having a good time."

"Edgar, I think my only chance of waking up is to go with the fellow."

"Fine. But I'm not going," he said.

Alma was silent. They sat waiting until the church tower began to strike midnight.

"I'm leaving!" said Alma, and she flew off.

Edgar never found out what became of Alma, or whether she woke up. He is a ghost to this day, and enjoying it very much. No doubt he has visited one of your Halloween parties if you live anywhere in the Western United States. Next year he plans to tour the Midwest.

GATHERING SNOWFLAKES

By Kendall Roman

Billy stared at the girl walking in grandma's front door. She had long blonde braids spilling out of her fur-lined hood. She smiled right at him, then looked away and walked past him, but she passed so close that he could practically breathe on the dainty freckles that traveled over the bridge of her delicate nose.

"You just wait right here by the fire, dear," said Grandma as she walked to the kitchen. "I know I've got some dates in the pantry."

"Thank you, Mrs. Mueller," said the girl in braids. She walked over to the fire, took off her mittens, and held her shapely little fingers out towards the warmth.

Billy watched, afraid to say a word and break the magic spell that had come over the house. He had seen other girls at school, but no one like this. He thought she was beautiful. Billy was ten years old, and had never had use for the word before. This feeling—which he now associated with the word *beautiful*—was new to him.

The girl said nothing but grew tired of holding her fingers out and withdrew them, beginning to look around the room.

Grandma came back into the living room with a covered dish. "There you are, dear. Tell your grandmother I've got more if she needs."

"Thank you," said the girl, putting on her mittens and grasping the dish.

"Billy, this is Mrs. Dayton's granddaughter, Rhonda. She lives down in the valley but she's visiting for the holidays. And this is my grandson, Billy. He lives with me here all the time.

And I'm lucky to have him, too."

Rhonda looked curiously at Billy and to his mind she looked unconvinced that anyone was lucky to have him. She seemed to squint a little when she looked at him, perhaps out of some minor distaste or disbelief. Actually she was slightly near-sighted, but this didn't occur to Billy.

Grandma opened the door for Rhonda, whose hands were now full, and she stepped out into the cold, clear night. "Hurry back and don't take a chill," said grandma. Rhonda walked briskly out with a hasty good-bye.

"Good-bye," said Billy softly.

Grandma bustled slightly heavily back into the kitchen and seemed to find forty-one tasks for Billy to do in the next half hour, but this was only to disguise her worry about what she had observed.

One cannot reach the age of sixty without noticing that certain stumbling blocks in life seem to trip up large numbers of people, regardless of their intelligence, wealth, rank, and overall intentions in life. In Billy's lingering attention on Rhonda, grandma saw the echoes of heartaches and unhappiness from ages past. If there was anything she could do to spare Billy from endless yearning and days of madness, she wanted to do it. But how does one caution another against a danger that cannot be perceived? If only it were as easy as the lesson she had given him on poison oak.

Grandma busied herself and Billy even more as the problem grew more confusing to contemplate. At last she could think of no other tasks to be done that evening. She and Billy sat together at the small kitchen table for their evening tea and cocoa.

"Grandma, it's snowing!"

Grandma looked out the window and a sudden inspiration hit her. "Yes, isn't it beautiful?"

she said. "So delicate. And so quiet."

Grandma got up and walked over to the window to gaze out at the snowfall. She motioned to Billy to come with her. They watched silently for a few moments. "Sometimes it's a good thing to admire something beautiful for a few minutes in your busy life." Billy looked up at her when she made this uncharacteristic statement. Since she continued to gaze out the window, he did likewise.

"What do you see?" she asked.

Billy looked at her again when she asked this unusual question, but he finally answered. "Snow. It's snowing."

"Do you like it?" she asked.

"Yes. I think I'll be able to go out and play in it tomorrow."

"Do you think it looks pretty?"

"I guess so," said Billy after a long and uncertain pause.

"I think it looks so pretty that I want to have some for myself." Grandma went to the cupboard and took out a dish, which Billy noted was exactly the same type that she had used for Rhonda's dates.

"Billy, will you go out and gather some snowflakes for me? Catch them coming down when they're nice and fluffy. Quick, put your coat and mittens on."

Billy did as he was told, though not without a few very amusing—to grandma—glances at her.

Within a few minutes he came in with a dish full of snow. Grandma received it with the utmost delight. "How beautiful! My very own snowflakes!" She put the dish on the kitchen table, then very slowly did the last of the day's dishes with Billy's help. When she was sure enough time had passed, she said to Billy, "Now let's sit down and enjoy the snowflakes."

With a perfectly straight face she approached the table and observed the dish of water. "Oh no! They're gone." She sat down anyway and looked at the dish with sadness.

"They melted, grandma. You waited too long," said Billy. Privately he wondered a little about grandma's soundness of mind.

"Well, everyone knows that snowflakes melt, don't they?" said Grandma sadly.

"They have some fake snowflakes that don't melt. Maybe you could get some of those, grandma."

"But it wouldn't be the same, would it?"

"No, I guess not," said Billy.

Grandma left Billy to ponder this episode and made no further comments.

The following Sunday was the date for the Christmas program at church, to be followed two days later by a Christmas Eve service and then finally Christmas Day. Billy had his hopes for Christmas, modest but definite. He never tired of putting together model airplanes of any type whatsoever, but he had made sure to point out to Grandma his absolute favorite, now for sale at the local craft store. It would have taken him several months of saving his allowance to buy it, but just maybe it would appear under the tree on Christmas morning.

He and Grandma had been alone for several years now, since Grandpa's death. Billy had never known his parents. Grandma had not yet seen fit to tell him the truth on that front, and fortunately he hadn't inquired.

The dress rehearsal for the Christmas program was on Saturday afternoon. Grandma drove Billy to the church with his shepherd costume. He was not doing this part for any other reason than grandma's silent expectation of him. It was part of the ritual one went through and he didn't wonder any deeper than that at its significance.

Billy heard concerned chatter among the adults in charge of the Christmas program and didn't bother to listen it. Delay in starting the rehearsal gave him more time to daydream about the new model airplane he expected on Christmas morning. Something made him turn his head, though, before it was time to start.

There she was. Rhonda was taking off her coat and sitting in one of the folding chairs with the girls. Billy realized with a mixture of horror and delight that she was going to take the place of Gracie, since Gracie had come down with a bad cold. Rhonda would play the part of Mary in the Christmas play. Mr. and Mrs. Dayton watched proudly as she sang the duet with Joseph. Even Billy noticed that she had a pretty singing voice.

After the rehearsal, Billy was caught off guard when Rhonda approached him and handed him a little wrapped package.

"My grandma told me to give you some date nut bread to take home," she said as she handed it to him. Billy looked several feet behind Rhonda and saw smiling Mrs. Dayton.

"Thank you," he said. Rhonda immediately turned around and he watched her being bundled up by her grandparents for the ride home. He didn't even notice the other boys teasing him about Rhonda. A little girl with soft brown hair had noticed, however.

"Hurry up now, Billy. I want to get home before the storm starts." He pulled on his coat and mittens, then trudged out to the parking lot with grandma. The snow was crunchy and dirty on the sides of the parking lot after three days of cold but no new snow. The air hung thickly and was a little warmer this evening. Billy noticed none of this. He even forgot his model airplane for the moment and relived the vision of Rhonda in his mind, wrapped in her Madonna robe. There was something about it that was almost painful when he thought of her, but it was such an unusual sensation that he continued calling up that vision.

Grandma hummed "It Came Upon a Midnight Clear" while she prepared their hot evening drinks. She was having warm eggnog instead of tea tonight, and Billy's hot chocolate had a candy cane in it. No sooner had he finished his hot chocolate when she announced, "The new snow is here. Shall we try gathering snowflakes again?"

"Don't you think they will just melt, grandma?" he said.

"No. We're going to put them in the freezer this time." Billy almost asked why she was so intent on gathering snowflakes, but grandma had such a dreamy expression on her face that it didn't look like she was open to answering any questions. "Get one of the dishes from the cupboard and gather some snowflakes for me, will you?" she asked.

He didn't mind doing that. He pretended that Rhonda was outside hiding in the snow and that he would find her. He had filled the dish just about half full with falling snowflakes when a car drove up.

It was not the Daytons' car. Mr. and Mrs. Kulander emerged, with their three children. The youngest was an infant sleeping on Mrs. Kulander's shoulder, and Billy recognized Sondra, who was about his age and had just been at the rehearsal. He walked behind a tree so as not to be noticed while they headed for the front door. He didn't know how he would explain gathering snowflakes to any regular person. Mr. Kulander was carrying a large covered bundle of some sort, and Billy finally recalled that the Kulanders had been bringing grandma a basket of Christmas goodies each year since grandpa had died.

Billy figured he would just wait out the Kulanders' visit before going back inside with the snowflakes. Unfortunately, grandma called out the front door for him just at that moment.

"Billy, have you got the snowflakes yet? Come in now, please. We have company."

Billy walked in the front door with the dish of snowflakes, and the Kulanders were exchanging such lively greetings with grandma that he was hoping not to be noticed.

"Ah, there they are!" said grandma. "Thank you, Billy. Snowflakes, some of the prettiest things on this earth." Grandma put them in the freezer, as she had said she would. "A little family ritual we're in the process of creating," she said parenthetically to the Kulanders, in case they were wondering.

"I think that's a great idea!" said Sondra enthusiastically. This was said with such sincerity that her mother smiled and lovingly stroked her soft brown hair.

"What do you do with the snowflakes later?" asked Mrs. Kulander.

"We haven't decided yet," said grandma mysteriously.

Sondra looked at grandma and then Billy with such admiration that he was impressed with grandma in spite of himself.

"And here is a small gift for you," said Mr. Kulander, unveiling his masterpiece. Mr. Kulander owned the local bakery. His Christmas cookies, sweet breads, and petit fours were a matter of great renown. People ordered them from all over the county and even from a neighboring state.

Grandma surveyed the basket with delight. She inspected each item and they all looked so inviting that it was enough to bring tears to one's eyes. She thanked him and he bowed with as much dignity as the conductor of a symphony might at the conclusion of a great work.

"Can I hab a pettafour?" said a tired voice. Everyone looked down at Tad, holding his mother's hand and eyeing his favorite item in the basket.

"No, honey, those are for Billy and Mrs. Mueller," said his mother.

"I think we might be able to spare one. What do you think, Billy?" said Grandma.

Billy answered by getting one of the petit fours out of the basket and handing it to Tad.

"Tanks," said Tad just a split second before he took the first bite.

"Would anyone else care to join him?" said grandma. "Come now, I insist. Family tradition."

Mr. and Mrs. Kulander split one of the cookies, while grandma took a slice of one of the sweet breads and Billy took a ginger snap. Sondra took an iced sugar cookie decorated as a snowflake, eyes twinkling. While the adults were chatting, Sondra came over to Billy and handed him a small present.

"I waited to give it to you here at your house so those boys wouldn't make fun of you," she said. Unfortunately her thoughtfulness was lost on Billy, since he hadn't heard the boys making fun of him about Rhonda.

"It's just a little something I made," she explained. "I feel so lucky to have my brothers and my mother and father, and I wanted you to have at least something. Merry Christmas, Billy." She smiled and actually gave him a little hug. Although he didn't return it, it made him wonder what it must be like to have a real family.

After the Kulanders left he discreetly opened the gift, alone in his room. It was a little stuffed dog, with buttons sewn on for eyes, a felt nose, and even a festive little collar around his neck. The tag said that his name was "Umbrage," with an explanatory note that she named him before she knew what the word meant. Even though umbrage means that somebody is feeling insulted, she didn't mean it that way and just thought it sounded like an interesting name for a dog. Billy put Umbrage in one of his drawers for now, because he wasn't sure that he wanted to explain anything to grandma.

The next morning, grandma retrieved the frozen snowflakes from the freezer during breakfast and set them on the table without comment. Billy looked at them. "They don't look like snowflakes at all any more, grandma," he said.

"You're right," she said, and she went to the sink and set them in the sink to melt. "But I'm not giving up yet. Maybe it will snow again tonight. We've no time to wonder about that now. We have some baking to do today—the cookies we'll be bringing to the Christmas program. Plus Mrs. Dayton has requested that you go over and help Rhonda practice for the show tonight."

Grandma watched closely for the reaction and there it was.

"Why doesn't Gary practice with her?" asked Billy, finally. Gary was playing the part of Joseph in the Christmas program.

"Well, I don't know exactly. But what Mrs. Dayton said is that Gary wasn't available today. For the life of me I don't know why Rhonda needs any practice, but this was a neighborly request and we're going to go over there at 2:00 this afternoon and oblige. Is that all right with you?"

"I guess so," said Billy with as much reluctance as he could pretend to put into his voice.

When the time came, Mrs. Dayton played the piano once for the duet while Billy painfully pretended to sing the part with her. Then she bustled grandma back to the sewing room to ask for her help in an alteration she was making in one of Mr. Dayton's vests. Mr. Dayton was apparently out shopping.

"Do you want to see my early Christmas present?" said Rhonda.

"Okay," said Billy.

Rhonda took Billy to her room and took a dress out of the closet. It was blue velvet with white lace. She held it up in front of her to show him how it might look on her. He was entranced.

"Grandma says it makes me look pretty," she said. "It's my Christmas dress."

Billy said nothing, only because he didn't know what to say. He watched Rhonda put the dress back in the closet. She adjusted it on the hangar and smoothed it lovingly, then turned and smiled at him.

 "Do you have any money?" she said.

What a curious question. He checked in his pockets and found three quarters left from his allowance and pulled them out of his pocket.

"Can I see it?" she asked. She held out her hand, and how was he to resist her request? He put the coins in her palm and watched them disappear into her pocket.

"You can't have them back until you kiss me," she said, with a hint of a smile.

Any self-respecting person would have recognized the injustice of that in a flash, but Billy was not in a logical frame of mind. He was immediately torn because on one hand it was a violation of the code of all young boys to even consider a girl would be worth touching in any way whatsoever. On the other hand, something mysterious was welling up in him. A few more moments, though, and fear of the unknown won out.

"You can keep it; it's okay," he murmured. He quickly turned to go back to the living room, but she grabbed his arm and barred his way out of her room.

"I'll show you how. I know all about it," she said.

Billy decided he really didn't want to participate in this venture, as kind as she was to offer up her knowledge, so it was extremely puzzling to him 20 seconds later that he had started and finished his first kissing lesson without having ever agreed to it. It happened too fast and the sensations were all so new and strange. It had also ended quite abruptly when Rhonda heard her grandmother walking across the second floor hallway toward the stairs. Rhonda backed away immediately, gave him his money and said, "Don't tell." Then she skipped out into living room, as carefree and innocent as a five-year-old, and was looking at a catalog before any adults emerged from the stairway.

Billy wondered at the rapidity with which Rhonda could shift gears. She now ignored him completely, as if nothing had happened at all and she had never noticed he existed.

At home again with grandma, they had a casual dinner and prepared for the Christmas program. It went very smoothly except for one thing that Billy was too dazed to notice. It would have meant the world to one kind-hearted little girl to know that her gift had helped Billy in some way to be happy. She waited for a glance or a smile from him, but there was none. He seemed more remote than ever. As she thought this over, a tear fell; not because she needed thanks or attention, but only because her mission had failed. She'd had such joy thinking it up, making Umbrage and naming him, and imagining what a companion he would be to Billy. But alas, her imaginings and efforts seemed to have been in vain.

After the Christmas program, new snow was falling. Billy knew grandma would ask him to gather snowflakes again. He was in a slightly sour mood because he didn't understand why Rhonda was completely ignoring him now and talking to another boy. Suddenly it dawned on him that maybe this other boy was going to receive a kissing lesson also, and he didn't like that idea at all. In fact, maybe it was happening right now. Rhonda had been talking to that other boy when he and grandma had left the church.

Grandma interrupted his musings by handing him the dish. "Gather some snowflakes, will you, Billy?"

"No. It's stupid. I'm not going to do it any more."

"Billy, what's the matter?"

"Nothing."

"Won't you please tell me what's bothering you?"

"What's bothering me is why you keep asking me to put snowflakes in a dish. How can you be so stupid?"

Grandma looked searchingly at him. "What happened, Billy?"

Billy suddenly froze. Did grandma know? How could she possibly know about that?

A terrible thought occurred to him. What if Rhonda had told her grandmother, and Mrs. Dayton told his grandma? That required immediate action, even if it was only a possibility.

"I have a headache. I'm going to bed," said Billy. He went to his room and closed the door. Grandma didn't bother him.

The thought of other people knowing what had happened between him and Rhonda was very troubling. What if the boys at school found out? That actually bothered him even more than the thought of Rhonda kissing other boys. He flew into a rage and could think of nothing better to do than throw the contents of his dresser all over the room, drawer by drawer.

Billy collapsed on his bed as his rage turned to bitter tears. He cried quietly for a few minutes. When he opened his eyes, there was Umbrage looking right at him. He'd forgotten all about the little stuffed dog he had put in his bottom drawer last night. He felt compelled to explain his actions to Umbrage by way of apology for the fact that he had tossed Umbrage against the wall. After all, Umbrage was not going to tell anyone else, nor was he going to reply with any sort of ridicule.

Umbrage sat quietly throughout the choppy explanation, didn't hold anything against Billy, and seemed to absorb it all quite well. Billy felt more level-headed, and wondered why he didn't feel more silly talking to a stuffed dog. The thing Billy was not aware of was the loving little girl who had granted so much life to Umbrage.

Umbrage seemed to indicate that it was time for Billy to put the contents of his drawers back in place, so Billy sighed and got busy. It wasn't until every last article of clothing was in its proper drawer that Billy realized he had to make a decision about Umbrage's permanent location. It seemed an injustice to put him back in the bottom drawer, so Billy looked about the room for a better spot. The more he thought about it, the more he thought Umbrage deserved the best spot in the place, which would be on the shelf with his model airplanes. It didn't even occur to Billy that grandma might notice and ask him about it.

At the same time, a wave of hope went through Sondra as she enjoyed Christmas cheer with her family a few miles away. She realized that maybe it would take Billy some time to get to know Umbrage and she shouldn't be disappointed just because he hadn't had an instant response. After all, that is how it was with people. It takes people time to get to know and love one another.

Billy's "headache" had been forgotten, so he indulged in a few moments of dreaming about the days ahead when he would have a new model airplane to assemble. After that he was hungry and went out to see what grandma might prepare for a bedtime snack. She was already making hot cocoa for him, thinking she would have to carry it to him in his room.

"Oh there you are. How's your headache?" she asked.

"Fine. I mean, it's gone."

Grandma, being a woman of good timing and patience, waited for Billy to ask the question. She had been waiting for several days and she thought it quite likely the question would come tonight.

"Grandma, why do you keep telling me to gather snowflakes?"

"It's my way of making a point, Billy."

Billy's forehead creased with noncomprehension.

"Snowflakes, like some of the other beautiful things in life, do not last," she said. "They can be admired as they fall from the sky, and even for some time as they lay on the ground, but the moment you try to have them, they are not what they once appeared to be.

"That is how it is with the things in life that we can touch, and see and feel. They seem to be the most real things, but they are not. They don't last. They change, they disappear, they serve their purpose and then become something else, like the food that you eat every day.

"There are some things that don't change. Trust, for example. You and I trust each other, don't we Billy?"

He nodded.

"You know I will take care of you every day, and I know you will come home from school and do your chores. You know that I care about you and you care about me.

"Honesty, truth, good intentions—these are the things you can count upon, and you should value them when you find them. You can't see them or touch them, but you can know they are there, and they are more real than anything.

"The confusing thing is that sometimes people—even people who seem to be beautiful, or privileged, or famous—are not honest and do not have good intentions. And when you try to have them in your life, it is like having a bowl of melted snowflakes. Actually it is worse because … it might be more as if the snowflakes turned to fire and burned your house down. Things happen that you don't expect, and they are most unpleasant."

Grandma stopped as she could see this was having an impact on Billy. Grandma, of course, did not know what had passed between Rhonda and Billy, but she rightly guessed that it was unpleasant.

Billy finally said, "Then we won't be gathering snowflakes any more, will we?"

"No."

Billy pondered this some before he fell asleep that evening. The next morning life seemed to be normal again. He got up and got dressed as usual and then noticed Umbrage on the shelf. Umbrage seemed to have something to say. Billy waited for a minute but he could not seem to understand what Umbrage was trying to communicate. He was just walking out of the room when he suddenly realized that Umbrage had been a gift to him, and he had not given a gift in return, which was the customary thing to do.

He turned back and asked Umbrage, "But how do I know what Sondra would like as a gift?" It seemed an impossible thing to know, especially since she was a girl.

Suddenly the image came to mind of her choosing the snowflake cookie, and the look in her eyes when she'd heard grandma talking about "gathering snowflakes." Billy conceived an idea and asked grandma to take him to the store to buy what he needed to make his gift.

On Christmas Eve, after the church service, Billy and grandma went to the Kulanders' to pay a visit. Billy brought his Christmas gift for Sondra and presented it to her. The whole family watched as she unwrapped and beheld a beautiful 3-D model snowflake, designed by Billy, complete with sparkles. The happiness it gave Billy to see his creation appreciated by someone other than himself was a new experience. Sondra hugged him, right in front of everybody, and this time he hugged her back and kissed her lightly on the cheek, surprising himself. It had nothing to do with the "kissing lesson" but only with what he felt.